One Monday morning in April 1916, the day after Easter, a boy and two girls set out from different places, each on their own separate journey to the centre of Dublin. They had no idea how their journeys would end.

Easter Monday, 1916, one of the most momentous and terrible days in the troubled history of Ireland, when a group of rebels try to wrest the government of their country from the might of the British Empire. Michael is determined to play his part in the historic events. His brother may be fighting for the British in the trenches of Flanders, but Michael will fight for his country's freedom—to the death, if necessary. Daisy is American, but her parents are Irish, and she is prepared to do anything for the cause—and girls can fight as well as men, for what they believe in.

Sarah just wants to be a nurse, to do her bit to help the wounded soldiers back from the battlefields in France, soldiers like her brother. But when the hospital in Dublin Castle gets caught in the uprising, Sarah finds her loyalties stretched to the limit. How can Irishmen be her enemy? She just wants to see an end to the killing, an end to the fear.

Elizabeth Lutzeier has worked as a teacher in Germany, America, and England. She has two of her own children and 1,300 children to keep her company most days in her work as headteacher of an 11–18 comprehensive school. Her first novel, *No Shelter*, won the Kathleen Fidler Award. Two of her books have been nominated for the Carnegie Medal and one for the Guardian Children's Fiction Award. *Crying for the Enemy* is her fifth novel for Oxford University Press.

Crying for the Enemy

Other books by Elizabeth Lutzeier

The Coldest Winter
The Wall
Lost for Words
Bound for America

Crying for the Enemy

Elizabeth Lutzeier

OXFORD
UNIVERSITY PRESS

OXFORD
UNIVERSITY PRESS

Great Clarendon Street, Oxford OX2 6DP

Oxford University Press is a department of the University of Oxford.
It furthers the University's objective of excellence in research, scholarship,
and education by publishing worldwide in

Oxford New York
Auckland Bangkok Buenos Aires
Cape Town Chennai Dar es Salaam Delhi Hong Kong Istanbul
Karachi Kolkata Kuala Lumpur Madrid Melbourne Mexico City Mumbai
Nairobi São Paulo Shanghai Taipei Tokyo Toronto

Oxford is a registered trade mark of Oxford University Press
in the UK and in certain other countries

British Library Cataloguing in Publication Data available

ISBN 0 19 275258 8

1 3 5 7 9 10 8 6 4 2

Typeset by AFS Image Setters Ltd, Glasgow

Printed in Great Britain by
Cox & Wyman Ltd, Reading, Berkshire

For Peter Lutzeier

Those that I fight I do not hate
Those that I guard I do not love

W. B. Yeats, 'An Irish Airman Foresees His Death'

Into the Darkness

One Monday morning in April 1916, the day after Easter, a boy and two girls set out from different places, each on their own separate journey to the centre of Dublin. They had no idea how their journeys would end. A volcano was about to erupt and cover their city with rivers of fire and they had no idea. Not even the boy, who'd practised being a soldier, marching for months with a broom handle over his shoulder instead of a gun.

Not even Michael knew what was going to happen that day as he crept down the wooden stairs from his bedroom and then across the yard to the barn in the pitch-black morning that felt like the middle of the night. He had no idea that by the end of the week he'd be lost in the dark and the choking smoke of heavy artillery fire, just like his brother out in the trenches fighting the Germans.

Michael managed to slip quietly out of the barn with the things he'd hidden there, the knapsack and the bits of his brother's army clothes he'd put together so he could say he had a uniform. He was almost clear of the barn when he froze. In the dead-of-night darkness of the yard he stiffened, as a sound like the shot of a single rifle tore open the morning. His breathing stopped. He waited for the cries. His mother screaming and crying for his brother, lost in the trenches in France. His father shouting at intruders, savage men with guns.

Nothing.

Michael started to breathe again and waited, still without

1

moving, for the animals to react to the sound he was sure would stop him setting off to Dublin that day. A noise like that was bound to have his parents up and about by now. For a split second he thought of giving up, of creeping round to the back stairs and getting himself back into bed. If his parents got to know he'd signed up with the Volunteers, they'd lock him in his room and watch over him every hour of the day. They wouldn't even let him go to church on his own if they had any idea he was off to fight like his brother. It wouldn't matter to them that it was the Irish Volunteers he'd joined and not the British army. They'd had enough of armies and fighting. His father said none of the fighting had anything to do with them. They didn't love the British and they didn't hate the Germans. They were just ordinary people like everyone else in their village, working hard and trying to make an honest living.

'The one bit of fighting they'll catch me doing is fighting to stop my two strong sons going off and getting themselves killed,' he'd said when the war started in 1914 and the priest had stood up in church and called for men to sign up and help the British in the war effort. He'd said the same thing in the pub a year later, the very first day he let Michael and Diarmid have a glass of cider between them, sitting on the wall outside. Then all his bold talk had been squashed and torn and spat out again, devoured by time as easily as one of those new harvesting machines devoured a whole field. Diarmid was already lost, somewhere out there in France, dead or still fighting the Germans. Michael felt the cool of the old stone wall on his forehead as he leaned forward and listened. He picked at the loose mortar in the barn wall, grazing his hands on the rough stones, waiting for his father to shout out at him to come inside. But there was no sound.

Then he smiled. What sort of a soldier was he going

to be, scared of a banging old door? Wasn't the loud crack he'd heard only the sound of the barn door slamming shut where he'd rushed out too quickly and not taken care to prop it open? His da always said he was to leave it open to get some more air to the animals inside. Michael carefully moved the great stone over to keep the door open and then inched his way round the back of the barn to get his bicycle.

He'd managed to get nearly everything the sergeant said they needed to bring along with them. He had the green jersey, an army one from his brother, and everything else except a gun. Michael knew he wasn't the only one with no gun and he at least had a real army knapsack, the knapsack Diarmid had given him the only time he was allowed home from wherever it was the British were fighting.

'Look after that for me and take good care of it.'

Diarmid was so much taller, looked so much older than Michael. That was how he had got away with signing up to fight for the British army a whole year earlier than he should have done.

'And don't let our mammy get her hands on it or she'll be washing it before you know where you are.'

Diarmid stretched out the thin straps to point out the two tiny stains on the coarse hemp handle as he whispered, 'That's the blood of a dead German.'

'Did you kill him?'

Diarmid shrugged his shoulders. 'You never can tell who you've hit. There's that much shooting and screaming going on. You wouldn't want to hear it.'

Michael had shown the knapsack with the specks of blood to all his friends—to everyone except his parents. They were set against Michael signing up for the British army even when he was old enough to fight.

'Anything but that!' his mother would say. 'Ireland's

not at war with anyone. Why are they getting young Irish boys to fight for the English? Let them fight their own battles.'

Diarmid once told Michael her sister had lost a son, a boy of twelve, in an ambush by the British army, over in the west of Ireland. But he couldn't be sure. His mother never spoke of her family in the west. All Michael knew was that the only time he ever heard his mother shout was when there was talk of war or of Michael going to be a soldier. Then she was fierce.

'Killing young lads your age. Younger than you. There's been enough fighting and killing in this country.' That was why Michael had kept the Volunteers secret, and the war they were going to fight one day against the British army in Ireland.

In his knapsack he had a small tin with a red cross on top—a first-aid kit he'd got from another Volunteer—and a quarter of the loaf his mother had made that night, with a lump of cheese squashed into a hole he'd made in the bread. They'd said to bring enough food for three days, but he couldn't have done that without his mother noticing. And anyway, most of the lads said Monday's meeting in Dublin was just for practising marching, and maybe to scare a few policemen. Not the real thing. There was no point in taking food for three days when he might well be home that night after his day in Dublin.

There was something wrong with his bicycle. Michael could feel the flat tyres straight away as soon as he started to move. He wheeled his bike slowly towards the gate, where the sun was painting the sky with red. The dogs would be barking soon. His da would be up for the milking. Michael bent down and felt the front tyre. No air at all. Completely flat. He took the pump from the bag on the back and bent down again to unscrew the valve.

It was missing. There was no valve on the back wheel either.

He stood up and looked at the house. The rising sun glittered on the darkened windows. So that was the game his da was playing. He remembered suddenly watching his da pumping up one of his tyres just before they went off to church on Good Friday and he'd wondered why the tyres could be flat again so quickly.

So that was the way they were trying to stop him joining up with the British army, trying to stop him leaving home. He had to go. He had to get off to Dublin. He was going to join up and be a soldier, whatever they did. They would be proud of him one day, fighting for Ireland.

He propped the bike up carefully against the gatepost just outside and closed the gate quietly behind him, not stopping to look back at the house again. It was going to be a long walk to Dublin.

It was Easter Sunday when Sarah told her father she didn't want to go back to her school in England because she wanted to get herself some real work. He smiled at her, his favourite.

'So you want to be one of these modern young women? A secretary or something like that?'

'I want to be a doctor, like you. But a doctor in a hospital.'

They were sitting in his study after lunch, watching a squirrel darting backwards and forwards across the lawn.

'You'll need to stay at school even longer if you want to be doctor. And there aren't many lady doctors, my dear. I don't know what your mother would say.'

Sarah pulled a face. The squirrel had found something

to eat and sat up, alert, as if it were watching the two of them sitting in the big bay window.

'Then I'll be a nurse. I am not going back to school. I've met girls in the hospital when I've been helping there, girls my age out working.'

She made a face again and pulled a pile of her father's pencils out of the tray, sorting out the ones that needed sharpening.

'I've got to do something. James is out there somewhere fighting. I can't just sit around reading books when everyone else is doing something for the war effort.'

Her father nodded.

'You *have* been going with your mother to the hospital, to help out.'

'That's not the same. We go there, we serve teas, and then we come home. And then I go back to school. It's not the same as being a proper worker for the war effort.'

Sarah's mother was the first woman in their district who had the idea of doing something for the war effort. And now, it was what all the ladies were doing. They started off with knitting, and then they began to have outings to Dublin Castle, to help to make tea for the men in the hospital there, all back from the fighting in France because they were wounded. Sarah's mother told her she was too young to help at first, said she didn't want her exposed to the horrors of war. And then one day, after she had got herself two nurse's outfits and Sarah was home for the holidays, she had taken Sarah with her.

The squirrel started off again, shooting all around the garden, as if someone had it on a wire and only needed to pull the wire to move it from one side to the other faster than they could follow it with their eyes.

'Look.' Sarah's father stood with his back to her

looking out at the garden and the hills beyond. Then he turned round. 'You have two more weeks of your holidays before you need to go back to school in England. I don't think it's a bad thing for you to see what it means to do proper work. I'll make you a promise. If you can manage a week, helping out at the castle hospital, I'll talk to your mother about you leaving school in another year or two. It's not a bad thing, these days, for a modern young woman to do some proper work before she gets herself married.'

Sarah didn't have to go to Dublin that Monday. She could have gone to the races with her parents and half of Dublin too. But she wanted to start as soon as possible and prove to her father that she wasn't too young to work. She was happy to do anything rather than sit in a row with her mother's friends and hear them discuss her complexion or her mother's plans for dresses.

The kitchen was warm and quiet on Monday morning in spite of Mrs Delaney's chatter. Sarah loved to take her breakfast there. In the dining room with her parents, she had to remember to sit up straight and wait to be served. In the kitchen she could help herself if she wanted. Mrs Delaney ladled thin porridge into a bowl, and Sarah helped herself to a spoonful of the best brown sugar, watching it melt into the hot porridge before she stirred it.

Mrs Delaney put butter and jam down next to the toast she had just finished making. It was six o'clock and the bright sun was throwing open the shutters on the morning. She blew out two of the candles on the kitchen mantelpiece and carried the third to the table. 'Come along now, my little Sally. Eat up. You've got to look after yourself if you're going to be looking after all them hungry young men.'

Her husband came in with wood for the range.

7

'Will you look at our little Sally here, Tom? Isn't she quite the young lady, in her nurse's uniform an' all?'

Tom Delaney shook the wood out into the basket and then gave the two little dogs a tickle along their backs before he turned round to look at Sarah.

'Aye, she'd look grand in anything. Wouldn't you be proud if she was your own daughter, all the work she's doing for the war?' He picked one of the dogs up by the scruff of the neck and moved it over to the other side of the fire.

'Well, I don't agree with all this war.' Mrs Delaney poured out a cup of tea, tipped some milk into it, and then pushed it across the table to her husband. 'A pretty girl like Sarah shouldn't have to be looking after young men who are half shot to pieces over some war with the Germans. What have the Germans ever done to us? Where's the sense in young Irish men getting themselves killed over anything at all? It's the English the Germans have got their quarrel with. I mean, I don't understand it, and that's a fact.'

Mr Delaney stood with his back to the mantelpiece and took loud sips of the hot tea. He glared at his wife and kept pointing at Sarah behind her back.

'Just as long as Mr James gets home safely. That's all that matters, eh, Miss Sarah. You'll want your brother back more than anything, now you're growing to a young lady. So's he can take you to all them dances and parties.'

He winked at Sarah and then grabbed his peaked cap with his left hand, taking one last gulp of his tea.

'I'm ready when you are, miss.'

He put his teacup down on the table and blew out the last candle.

'The motor's been running a treat these last few days. You'll enjoy the ride into Dublin, miss. But we'd better be off, so I can be back in time to get your mother and father to the races.'

Daisy Healey had had enough. Enough of Ireland and nuns. Enough of her new school where she was as good as buried alive. She had written out her complaints every day in her diary, carefully recording what she had done so she could talk about it when she next saw her family. Then on Monday, 24th April, Daisy wrote the longest entry she had ever made. It was the long, long letter she wanted to write to her parents but couldn't send. She didn't know where they were, so there was no point in writing them a letter, and yet she had to say something, had to let someone know what she was feeling.

So she wrote in her diary about the quiet of the place. She was going mad, she wrote, with the quiet nuns, the quiet of the convent school when the girls were off on their Easter holidays, the quiet crying every night of the two Polish sisters at the end of her dormitory. The need to be quiet all the time was quietly driving her mad. And she missed life in the open air since her parents had brought her over from America and left her at the school at the beginning of March. She wrote that the only fresh air they got was their daily walk, in a long crocodile, through the Dublin streets. She wrote about how much she missed the countryside outside Boston, and her grandfather's farm, where he'd taught her to shoot and told her she was better than any boy he'd ever had to teach.

Writing in her diary was better than any letter. It was almost as good as sitting and talking to a good friend, to someone like her grandfather who always wanted what was best for her. And as she wrote she gradually realized that she could do something to get herself out of the convent in Eccles Street and back home. It didn't even matter that she was no longer sure where her parents were, that all she knew was that they were somewhere in Ireland on some sort of business. That didn't matter. She could send her grandfather a telegram. He would find a way to get her home. The main post office was just down the road from the convent school in Eccles Street; they passed it almost every day on their walks with the nuns.

Daisy's mind was made up. She didn't want to stay in the convent any longer than she could help it. She even knew what her telegram would say. There was no point in waiting until the nuns took them out for their afternoon walk. Daisy knew she wouldn't be allowed out of the group to go to the post office on a Monday: Thursday was post day. She knew she was going to get herself in trouble whatever she did, so she decided she might just as well get herself in really big trouble and go out for a walk on her own. Daisy looked at the last thing she had written in her diary.

'Ireland good. Sad at school. Please bring me home. Daisy.'

She closed the black book with its red binding and put it into the deep pocket of her dark woollen coat. The two Polish girls were the only other pupils still left in school that holiday weekend. They sat with their backs to Daisy at the opposite end of the dormitory, reading together in their very sad voices. Daisy, in the new white dress her mother had bought her to wear on Sundays and holidays, picked up her coat and crept behind them out of the door of the dormitory. They didn't notice her leaving.

She moved quickly. The long, dark corridors, the stairs, the entrance hall, all were empty and quiet. The sister on duty at the front door had slipped outside to talk to her niece who was on her way back from mass. Daisy walked out, flung her coat around her shoulders, remembered she'd forgotten her hat and just grinned. That was another thing they'd shout at her for when she got back to the convent after sending her telegram. No girl was ever allowed out without a hat. She smiled again. She was free. She had found a way of getting herself back home to America and nothing was going to stop her. She strode out into the sunshine on her way into the centre of Dublin, the day that freedom set fire to the city.

1

There was a flash of bright, white light in the dark, and an echoing crash. Like lightning. Or a gunshot. It was one of the massive, heavy doors of the General Post Office being opened quickly—just a crack—and then closed so it clanged in the lock.

A girl had slipped inside. Just walked in off the street. Into the dark, barricaded building from the brilliant sunshine outside. As if it were a normal day. As if the world would ever be normal again. As if you could just walk into the post office and buy a stamp on a day like that.

Michael heaved the rifle up onto his shoulder and touched the trigger. Not enough to shoot. They'd told him to shoot anyone who came in. On sight. But he couldn't shoot her. They couldn't mean that he was supposed to shoot women and girls. His hands shook. They'd told him to almost close one eye to take aim, but he couldn't see properly when he did that. Specks of dust made bright lights, floating just beyond his field of vision. He looked at the girl. He couldn't shoot her. He wasn't a coward, but he couldn't shoot a girl in cold blood, just like that. She had shining, silver-blonde plaits and because her black woollen coat was open, her white, Easter holiday dress shimmered in the darkness of the shuttered entrance hall.

Michael rushed forward, waving his rifle. 'Get out of here. Get out. Get out. We want the English out of here. We're clearing everyone out.'

12

He waved his rifle, but she didn't move. Just stared at him as if he was out of his mind. He went right up to the girl and pushed the rifle at her arm. He had to get her out. If he didn't shoot her, someone else would. He grabbed at the sleeve of the long dark coat she was wearing.

'The post office is ours now. It's our land. Our buildings. Our city. Go back to filthy England, if that's where you belong.'

The girl was used to the sudden darkness now. She pulled her coat slowly out of his clenched fist and slowly pushed aside the German Mauser rifle so that it was pointing at the floor. Then she kicked him in the shin, laming him with a pain that forced him to drop the gun.

'I am *not* English.'

She picked up the rifle, slinging it over her shoulder by its leather strap.

'And anyway, you're not old enough to carry a gun like this.'

She pushed open the swing door behind him and strode along the whole length of the post office hall under the high, shuttered windows before she whirled round and whispered, 'Just what are you all here playing at?'

Behind the two of them, right at the back behind the counter, frightened clerks were packing away, counting money, counting stamps, refusing to leave their posts until everything had been accounted for. A group of other soldiers, older than Michael, were standing over the counter clerks, watching their hands, with orders to shoot if anyone made a sudden move to a drawer or cupboard. The girl seemed to become aware all of a sudden that the darkened post office was full of soldiers. Not of people sending letters and telegrams. How could it be? It was a holiday. A bright April day. The people of Dublin were all out enjoying themselves.

Michael stood three paces away from the girl, marking her. He probably wouldn't have been able to use the rifle anyway. He'd never learned to use a gun. But he thought he could knock her down if she tried anything. She was calm, taking time to look at everything that was going on. First at one anxious counter clerk, piling the counted money into slots in a wooden box. Then at the young soldier hanging over him, so scared he looked as if he were just about to be sick.

With the gun hanging over her shoulder, no one tried to stop the girl moving about the room. Soldiers stopped to look at her. They smiled at the stranger, with her white-blonde plaits and her bright, white dress, but nobody tried to stop her going wherever she chose. Only Michael kept a close eye on her, following her round and reminding her at every move that she was supposed to leave with all the other civilians.

The girl started to move up the first flight of stone stairs towards the telegram desk, where a group of soldiers were standing over the women there. Four of the women were standing, hats and coats on, handbags over their arms, ready to leave the building. But there was one woman who refused to leave her post, the Scottish woman in charge of the telegraph office.

'I've got messages I've been trusted to send. News of deaths and births. There's a young man getting married in Nottingham today and the mother couldn't be there. I've got to make sure my messages go out.'

'That's what I'm here for,' said Daisy.

The group around the telegram desk, soldiers and clerks, turned to look at the American girl with the long, blonde plaits, standing under the shuttered window on the first landing.

The woman at the telegram desk smiled for the first time.

'See, that's why I'm needed here. I can't leave my post. There's people want messages sent every minute of the day.' She pointed to the girl. 'Now put that gun down, dear. You're not old enough to carry a gun. And it doesn't suit a young lady from the convent.'

The telegram woman sat down. The four other women and the soldier who had started to move them over towards the stairs, holding his gun like a spade over his shoulder, edged slowly back to where the American girl was now the centre of attention.

Daisy sighed. Sometimes she felt she had been abandoned, like an orphan, on the steps of the convent school in Eccles Street on that afternoon in March when she had last seen her mother and father. They'd arrived at the school too late to take her out to meet her aunt and cousins just outside Dublin. Too late to spend Easter anywhere else but with the nuns. The women in the post office knew her as the girl whose parents were somewhere away on business.

'I know who you are,' the telegram woman said. Then she told everyone else. 'She's just arrived at the convent in Eccles Street. Daisy, her name is. But the rest is top secret. Her father and mother are doing some work for the American government, in Paris we think, but the telegrams go to somewhere in the West of Ireland first. It's all ever so secret, but that's why she needs to send them a telegram every week, on a Thursday usually, to tell them she's well. Those were my instructions from the reverend mother. That's why I can't desert my post, whatever you gentlemen say.'

She held out both her hands to the circle of soldiers crowding round her desk.

'And that's why I'll get your message sent, young

lady, as quick as a flash, so you can be out of here and back to the convent where it's safe.'

Daisy hitched the rifle up on her shoulders. She smiled. Everyone was looking at her. 'I've got cousins somewhere near Dublin. My parents made me stay here instead of going with them to wherever they've gone, because they said it was safer, here in Dublin. I want to send a telegram to Boston today, not the West of Ireland.' She pushed her way towards the woman and leaned over the desk, grinning.

'Hey, I know. You ought to write, "Am surrounded by soldiers. Stop. Locked in the GPO. Stop. Don't worry. Stop. Got a gun. Stop." Why don't you write that?'

The group of soldiers around the desk was growing. The telegram woman stood up again. 'Just a minute. Be patient, please, if you don't mind. I've got to look up Boston. I don't do Boston more than twice a week.'

A voice cut through the chaos on the first floor landing and echoed down the stairs. 'To your posts. Clear this hall.'

At the curve of the stone steps between the first floor and the second, a man in the peaked cap of an officer, pistol in his right hand, raised his left hand to slow the descent of a group they had found upstairs, a group of seven British soldiers. The British army sergeant in charge of them had his hand pressed against his forehead, but not hard enough to stop the blood flowing down his face and over his shoulder.

No one moved. The telegram women clutched their handbags tightly and looked from the officer to their supervisor and back again.

'That's Mr Pearse.' Michael pulled down his brother's old green jersey and straightened his father's brown belt, the only bits of uniform he had. Then he whispered again. 'General Pearse. Commander-in-chief.'

16

One of the general's men stepped out from the group and walked to the telegram desk. The soldiers round the desk moved aside, leaving Daisy still waiting for her message to be sent. He opened the little wooden door at the side of the desk and waited for the Scottish telegram woman to leave her post.

'I am afraid I am going to have to ask you to leave, miss.'

'I will not. There are messages to be sent. Don't ask me to go, sir.'

'The Volunteers will take over all messages that need to be sent, miss. The GPO is no longer the property of the British government. We will make sure all your messages get through.'

'And what about my message?'

The officer looked for the first time at Daisy. She smiled and hitched the gun up over her shoulder. 'I need to send a message to my grandfather to tell him I'm safe.'

The officer shook his head. 'No non-essential communications. We do not tell the outside world what our strength is. And it is better for families not to know your whereabouts in case they're questioned.' Then he took Daisy by the shoulders and took her under the windows where the shutters still let in some light.

'You're not a Volunteer. How old are you?'

Daisy glared at Michael, still marking her from several paces.

'As old as that boy over there. And I can handle a rifle better than him. I *am* a Volunteer if you'll let me stay.'

'Sir, she shouldn't be in here,' Michael said. 'She only came in to send a telegram.'

But the officer had already been called away to where the British soldiers were being lined up and made to lie down on the floor. There was still noise and confusion as the last of the post office workers were rushed down the stairs towards the doors.

'You ought to go too,' Michael whispered. 'Get out of here while there's still time. This is no place for a girl.'

But that wasn't true. There were other girls and women there as Volunteers. Some had armbands with a red cross on. Some had rifles. The only thing that made Daisy look out of place was her bright white dress and silver-blonde plaits when the other women were dressed in serious combat green and had their hair neatly tied back. Daisy stopped at last and turned on Michael, smiling.

'I know who you are! You're the Sinn Feiners, aren't you? Fighting for Ireland? My father works for Ireland and my grandfather too back home in Boston. Well, you need people who can shoot, and I can shoot. There's nobody else here is telling me to go. So I'm staying. I can't telegraph my parents to tell them I'm safe, so they're going to worry about me from Thursday on. The nuns will miss me today, but my parents won't really miss me until next Thursday. I'm staying.'

She smiled again and took the gun off her shoulder, pointing it towards one of the large, shuttered windows and looking along the barrel.

'You're too young.' Michael held out his hand to take the rifle from her. 'You really ought to go.'

'Listen to you. How old are you, Mr Sinn Feiner? What on earth brings you here, when you don't know one end of a gun from the other?'

'I do too.'

'You don't either.'

The two of them were standing near the bottom of the stairs, still arguing, while the last of the workers

18

cleared the building. In the middle of all the noise, they were whispering.

'Go on. What are you doing here?'

'I'm Irish.'

'So are half these people being forced out. You'll need a better story than that, Sinn Feiner.'

'My brother's in France, getting himself killed for the British. I'm fighting for my country. Which is why you've no business to be here. You're not Irish. You're American.'

'Tell that to my father. He's as Irish as *you* are. And my grandfather too.'

Daisy turned and walked a few paces away from him.

Nobody was guarding the door; she could have just walked out. That's what Michael wanted her to do. It wasn't that he really wanted her to go, but he didn't want her to stay around and get hurt. Because that was what people said was going to happen. They were all going to get themselves killed. At every meeting of the Volunteers they had heard that they were going to die, fighting for their country. Michael knew that he was going to die. And that was all right if they were all proud of him after that. The girl too, the American girl. Dying for his country would be worth it, if that made him a hero to a girl like that. But she didn't deserve to get herself killed for Ireland. A girl who'd just wandered in off the streets to send a telegram.

Then Michael came up with another good reason to make her leave. What if she was a spy? She had an American accent, but that didn't mean she couldn't be helping the British. She was still taking her time, looking into everything that was going on. She could easily be a spy for the British.

Michael looked round for help. He only took his eyes

off her for a split second and suddenly she was right there, jabbing his side with the gun.

'Here, you can have your gun back.'

Daisy took the rifle strap off her shoulder and started to walk backwards, back towards the stairs.

'Those English soldiers have got guns I can have. That German one you've got is one of those that leaves great big bruises on your shoulders every time you fire. You can keep it.'

Michael was angry with her. She thought she was the bee's knees, all her talk about guns. And how should she know all she made out to know? A girl from the convent school. He took the rifle and moved back to the post he had been given the minute the Volunteers entered the building. He wanted to prove to Daisy at least that he was a proper soldier. He had been told to guard the door and he had left his post. No one was guarding it now. He realized there must be soldiers outside, starting to secure the building. They had opened the huge outer doors again and the sunlight streamed in from outside. A man came through the inner swing doors, another civilian.

'Stop. Who are you?'

Michael blinked as he confronted the bright sunshine. He didn't know what he was doing. He could hardly see the man, let alone shoot him. It was all madness. He didn't know what he was supposed to do and the light made him feel sick. They couldn't really want him to shoot anyone who walked in.

His brain was splitting into little pieces. He wanted to get away. He wanted to stay there and die a glorious death for Ireland. He wanted to go back home and help his father get the cows in for milking before it was too late that evening, before his parents realized he had joined up. He wanted to hold the post office against the hordes of British soldiers garrisoned in Dublin, firing to the last, even after he was wounded. He wanted to make sure that Daisy got safely back to her school in Eccles Street. He wanted Ireland to be free. He wanted to go back to the day before, to mass on Easter Sunday when they had prayed for Ireland. He had felt proud and happy then, knowing that one day he would fight for his country and freedom because only the week before he had been properly accepted as a Volunteer.

He wanted to go back to their arrival in Dublin that morning when, sick with excitement, he'd realized they were being called up to fight that day. He wanted to meet Daisy somewhere else—not in the middle of a rebellion but in Bewley's Coffee House, at his school, at church. He wanted to be with Daisy, to talk to her somewhere far away. That was all he knew. That he didn't want to be there, where he was, at the door of the GPO, with orders to shoot.

He prodded with his rifle at the man who had just walked through the door and shouted at him.

'Stop, I said. You have no business here.'

'I only wanted to buy some stamps, mate.'

'Get out of here.'

He pushed at the man, who staggered backwards, dropping the hat he had been carrying.

'All right, mate. All right.'

The man, who was smaller than Michael, picked up his Homburg hat, clapped it on his head and walked slowly away, under the portico out at the front. Michael blew out, relieved that he hadn't had to shoot the man, then hitched his gun over his shoulder, patting the handle.

'Is it loaded?'

Daisy had taken her coat off and stood with her own rifle at his elbow.

'You shouldn't creep up on people like that. Especially not when there's a war going on.'

'No. You've got to learn how to make sure no one creeps up on you.'

Daisy looked straight along the barrel of her rifle, pointing it straight at Michael, and pulled the trigger.

'Not loaded.'

She grinned.

'Can you believe that? They've just finished disarming the British soldiers. Seven of them set to guard the post office. And none of them had any ammunition. Can you believe that?'

She pulled the trigger again.

'They said they never have any. No call for it on a normal day.'

She burst out laughing.

'Now just imagine, if the whole British army in Ireland never has any ammunition, there's no problem.'

A sergeant stopped beside them, and stared at the girl laughing in the sunshine at the entrance.

'There's work to be done, youngsters. You mustn't stay around here if you just want to laugh and have a good time. There's nobody having a good time in France at the moment. Here.' He pointed to Michael. 'You, young lad. You go and help to open all the window shutters. Then they'll be wanting you to smash the glass out. Got a good, strong handle on your rifle?'

Michael nodded. 'Yes.'

The sergeant raised an eyebrow and waited.

'I have got a good, stout handle. Sir.'

The sergeant gave Daisy a sack full of handbills.

'You, young lady. Hand these out to the people passing by.'

Daisy saluted. 'Yes, sir.'

Then, as soon as he had moved away, she pulled one of the papers out and started to read it aloud.

'The Provisional Government of the Irish Republic. To the People of Ireland.'

She waved the paper at Michael.

'Will you listen to that? That's why we're here. Doesn't this sound grand? Listen.'

She read on, whipping one of her long, blonde plaits over her shoulder when it got in her way.

> 'IRISHMEN AND IRISHWOMEN: In the name
> of God and of the dead generations from which
> she receives her old tradition of nationhood,
> Ireland, through us, summons her children to
> her flag and strikes for her freedom . . . '

She pulled out another handbill and shoved it at Michael.

'Look. Look. That's why we're here. Why would you want to be anywhere else? Who would want to be anywhere else on a day like this?'

Daisy strode out into the sunshine and Michael watched her for a short while as she wandered up and down along the whole length of the GPO under the great portico fronting on to Sackville Street. Everyone stopped and took one of her handbills off her, as she smiled and chatted and twirled in her white dress. Michael followed the sergeant inside then, helping to open the huge, heavy shutters. At every window he saw Daisy again, waving to him, showing him how she had nearly given away all her handbills, pulling faces whenever the sergeant's back was turned.

The whole main hall of the GPO grew lighter and Michael was able to see the British soldiers under guard. There was an argument going on. He could see people's faces, though he didn't catch the words. A young woman with a red-cross band on her arm was holding a bandage up to the British sergeant's head, where he had been grazed by the only shot they'd so far had to fire.

Jimmy Walsh, the other young soldier doing the shutters, pointed at the wounded man.

'He's a Scot,' he said. 'My uncle's a Scot and they can be awful stubborn. He won't go off to the hospital to get himself done up. They say he must have gone a bit crazy, like, from France. They've all been in France, the British soldiers. He keeps on saying the same things. Saying he's on duty till six to guard the GPO and he won't desert his post till then.'

'Ah, he ought to go and get himself seen to,' Michael said. 'They've got a hospital up at the castle now, haven't they? I think my da told me as that's where they're putting all the bad cases they bring back from France. They ought to take him off there to get his wound sorted. And they ought to keep him there until he's well in the head again.'

At the far end of the main hall, near to the entrance, Volunteers had started to smash the windows, making the glass shatter onto the pavement outside. Daisy had finished with all her handbills and moved towards the door. At the window, Michael watched her.

She held her empty sack upside down and shook it, although there was nothing left to fall out. Then she rolled up the sack and stood there, twisting and untwisting it into a plait, staring across the wide street to the grand shops and hotels on the other side still basking in the bank holiday sunshine. Michael wanted to ask her what she was thinking but the sergeant came up behind him and the other Volunteers.

'Come on, lads. There's two windows still to be done. And then we'll need those mailbags over there for barricades. Look lively.'

24

Michael took the stout, wooden handle of his rifle and smashed his first pane of glass. Then they punched and smashed and crashed the windows in till all of them were broken.

2

Sarah always looked forward to arriving at the gate of Dublin Castle, where the policemen saluted her. The police on duty saluted everyone in uniform and she always arrived wearing her mother's nurse's uniform. That was what all the volunteers wore, even though none of them were real nurses, even though none of them had ever done a proper day's work in their lives. Sarah's mother, like all the other ladies, was proud to be doing her bit for the war effort. She enjoyed making tea once a week for the poor men invalided home from Belgium or France.

'The rooms at the castle are such very nice rooms for the poor soldiers,' she used to say. 'And the men are so very grateful.'

The policemen at the gate knew Sarah better than they knew her mother. Whenever she was home from school for a holiday, she would find that her mother had volunteered and then just couldn't manage to get to the castle on the day she had a duty.

'They love you so much up there,' she used say, patting Sarah's cheek. 'They're so grateful to see you. A young girl like you, with your pretty dark hair under your nurse's cap. A uniform really quite suits you, my dear.'

Sarah was glad to get away. She liked talking to her father but he was busy at his surgery for a lot of the time she was at home; her brother was fighting in France; and her mother's friends were boring.

'Good morning, my dear.'

The policeman at the gate saluted and stood to

26

attention. He was older than Sarah's father, older and much rounder. One or two army sentries hung around chatting in the yard, but they were not quite as important. Sarah's friend the policeman was the one people had to get past if they wanted to make their way into the castle and the hospital. Her brother, James, had enjoyed trying to frighten Sarah with all the harsh things he had to say and do on sentry duty when he was doing his army training in England, but the policeman at the castle gate wasn't harsh like real soldiers. Sarah had never heard him being strict with anyone. The nurses said he wouldn't hurt a fly.

The hospital wards in the castle were quiet, the men who could sit up smiling and waving as she made her way down the middle of each room past the rows of beds.

'Good morning, little nurse.'

She liked the soldiers calling her 'nurse'; it reminded her every time that her mother had told her a real lady should never think of that sort of occupation. Her mother had other plans for her life.

'There won't be time for you to work after you've left school, my dear. You'll be so busy after you're married. Just wait and see. It's a very good thing for now, of course. Helping out with the war effort and so forth. A young man respects a woman for that, you know.'

'A beautiful young lady like you should be out in the sunshine on a day like this. Not stuck in the gloom with the likes of us.'

A soldier limped past her, smiling, showing his bright, white teeth in a thin, sun-tanned face. He was obviously one of those who were well enough to get out into the garden and the yard, in spite of his crutches. Sarah remembered taking tea to him on the wards when he had been too ill to get up. Even then he had been smiling.

She smiled back at him and hurried on. She was late now, but soon she had an excuse for her lateness. Matron stopped her in the corridor and introduced her to a tall, elegant woman with silvery blonde hair.

'Sarah is the only young volunteer who has joined us today.'

The woman shook Sarah's hand.

'And Sarah certainly hasn't got an American accent.' Matron guided them both back down the stairs towards the main entrance. 'I assure you, I would know if we had a new volunteer, if your daughter were here with us, especially a girl with an American accent.'

On the steps, matron promised the woman she would contact her if there was any sign of her daughter and then walked back into the building with Sarah.

'The poor woman. She arrived in Dublin to take her daughter out for the day from her boarding school and the girl's disappeared. The nuns have lost her. Now they've told Mrs Healey to search the hospitals. She thinks that means they want her to look for young volunteers like you. Never a thought that the girl may have run away out into the countryside for good and all. Well, I hope she finds her soon, Lord love her. You wouldn't want to lose your only child, now would you? I don't have any children myself but I know we'd all be frantic if one of my sister's children went missing.'

Sarah's first job was to help with clearing up the ten o'clock lunch dishes. Most of the volunteer helpers had stayed away on account of the Easter holidays, so Sarah was alone in the kitchen with Kitty Walsh, who had done with school and was training to be a nurse. It hardly mattered that there were so few of them. They wouldn't have needed the extra American girl even if she had turned up looking for some work to do. The hospital was quiet. Most of the men were already starting to get better

28

by the time they arrived here; Sarah had never known one of them die in the whole of the year she'd been helping. The soldiers were brought to the castle to get better, not to die.

She tied up the sleeves of her dark blue dress with the bands frilled around elastic and put a striped, blue-and-white kitchen apron over the starched white one Mrs Delaney had laid out that morning. Sarah had to hitch up the dress and apron with a broad belt because her mother was still a good five inches taller than her. She stood on a box to reach down into the deep sink and plunged her hands into the boiling water. Kitty pulled down one of the stiff, white linen cloths from the pile and stood ready to start with the drying.

'You remember Major Watts last week, don't you, Sarah?'

Sarah frowned and dumped three steaming wet tea plates at once onto the draining board.

'Who's he? I don't do high-up officers. It's only the important volunteers get to serve them. How do you know a major?'

'You do know him. The one in a room on his own, the one you have to walk past on the balcony. When you go down that slope to the supper kitchen.'

Kitty knew the castle better than anyone. Her father had worked as a policeman there before he had been sent out to France. She'd been in and out of the place since she was tiny and had been the first girl to go there as a volunteer, when she was twelve.

Sarah frowned again. 'I don't know any Major Watts.'

'You do too. Two broken legs and the side of his face with hundreds of stitches. He can't eat on his own so he has to be fed.'

'He's not died, has he? We've never had anyone dying here. At least, not so long as I've been a helper.' Sarah sighed and dumped some more tea plates with a crash onto the draining board. 'Would you believe it? I've never seen a dead person. My mother thinks it's not right for a young girl to see a dead body. But if he is dead, really dead, there's no reason why I shouldn't see him. I'm old enough now. I'm not a baby.'

'Nah.' Kitty dried the dishes faster than anyone, and threw them up onto the long shelves around the scullery. 'No, he's not dead.' She laughed and stretched up to get herself another drying cloth. 'He's the opposite of dead, that's what he is. He got awful lively in the middle of the night. So lively they had to bring some men up from the yard to hold him down.'

Sarah pushed her black hair out of her face with the back of her soapy hand.

'But he can't move, can he? You said he had two broken legs.'

'That didn't stop him. He kept trying to get out of bed. He would have broken his legs again, they said. He didn't know what he was doing. And he was screaming and screaming about shells and lights and telling people to get back. He kept shouting at them to put the lights out even though it was pitch dark. And when they got hold of him he was burning hot and dripping wet with sweat.' Kitty dipped her hand into the deep sink full of hot water and held it up against Sarah's face.

'Like that. Feel that hand. That's the state he was in.'

Sarah laughed. 'I know what hot water feels like.'

'Four men had to hold him down. And then they wrapped him tightly in blankets—like you do with babies—and after an hour or two he was quiet and went to sleep.'

They carried on washing and drying. The great clock on the landing outside ticked towards the chimes for eleven o'clock.

'You'd think he'd be ashamed of himself, an' all,' Kitty said. 'A grown man like that screaming like a baby. I mean, they took care of his wounds weeks ago. He must have got used to the pain. He's been here at the castle for a month.'

'What if my brother gets wounded? I wouldn't like to see James in the state some of them are in here. Maybe it's better if they get themselves killed. You know, maybe it's better to be dead than like he is with hundreds of stitches in his face.'

Kitty had slowed down with her drying and Sarah tried to balance one more plate on the pile already on the wooden draining board. The whole pile started to slide and both girls caught the plates from either end and laughed as they stopped them falling.

'I don't think my daddy'll get himself wounded,' Kitty said. 'At his age, they'll be putting him on sentry duty, not in the trenches. It's in the trenches they all say they've been hit.' She sighed. 'I pity their mothers, myself.'

'And their wives,' Sarah said. 'What if you've just got yourself married? And then he goes out to France to fight the Germans with the British army and the next thing you know he's in Dublin Castle hospital, all shot to pieces.' She shuddered. Then she rolled her sleeves up as far as she could, reached down into the deep water and pulled the plug out. On the range, the two kettles they had set to boil for fresh, hot water were whistling and steaming away.

'That's why James didn't get himself engaged to Victoria Coles. He said it wouldn't be fair on her if he got himself shot.' Sarah patted at the soap suds still left in the sink and wiped her hands across the blue and white striped apron. 'But he's going to be all right. I know James. He'll just make sure he doesn't get himself shot. That's all there is to it.'

Two of the nurses arrived with a trolley.

'You've earned yourselves a cup of tea, young ladies. Come and get it. We've settled the men in the wards and matron says we can sit down for a while, so we're going out to the balcony.'

As they moved outside from the dark, windowless corridors into the sunshine, they passed a row of single rooms that opened onto the outside walkway towards the balcony. Kitty jerked her head backwards into one of the rooms. Through the open doors, Sarah could just make out the sleeping figure, well wrapped up.

'That's the major,' Kitty whispered. 'He looks all right now. But you should have heard him last night.'

'You weren't here last night.'

'I know, but I heard about it. Everyone was talking about it this morning.'

Sarah sat down with her tea and grinned, listening to the other volunteers talking away. She was among friends here in the castle. She felt at home. And she had a whole week of staying here to prove to her father that she was grown-up enough to leave school early.

'Come quick. They're setting fire to the castle.'

The man ran off, away down the corridor, and shouted out into the next room.

'Come quick. They're setting fire to the castle.'

It was just after twelve.

In the supper room kitchen a whole row of kettles steamed and whistled away on the range. But there were no teapots in there in the morning. There were strict instructions to save all the hot water for washing bandages, one of the jobs they gave to the younger volunteers.

Sarah felt as if her face was on fire, with all that steam and her hands in hot water for the last two hours.

She was desperate for any excuse to get out of that room where the only windows were frosted glass so high up near the ceiling that she could hardly reach them even by standing on the table. She and Kitty ran to the next room to look out of the window. But all they saw was an empty yard. No sign of fire or anybody firing.

The great clock chimed for 12.15 and they rushed back to their work. They had to hang the bandages up to dry before they could help to lay tables and prepare ward trays for the men's dinner. There wasn't time to chase round after rumours and there was no sign of smoke. They were talking a load of nonsense or someone had been having a joke about the castle being on fire.

Sarah hung the blue and white striped apron on the back of the door to the supper room kitchen and ran along the corridor to the first ward to help lay the trays. Mary, one of the proper nurses, ran in, late back on duty, and looked round for matron. When she saw that her lateness wasn't going to be noticed she joined Sarah setting out the trays.

'There's trouble,' she whispered, 'down in O'Connell Street. They say the Sinn Feiners have taken the post office. They say they're going to storm the castle.'

Sarah reached over and straightened out the twisted straps on Mary's apron. She was hardly listening to the words. She'd heard it all before, people sounding the alarm about the rebels.

'You're going to get into terrible trouble with matron, if she sees you looking like that.'

'The policeman at the gate says everyone's making a fuss about nothing. But I've heard for a certainty we're all going to be killed. If those Sinn Feiners get their hands on the castle, we're all going to be killed straight away. Anyone who works for the government. What'll we do?'

She swatted at the tears on both sides of her face,

but still they kept coming. She grabbed a handful of knives and clanged them down on the trays, counting them out and using the hospital routine to calm herself down.

'We'll be as right as rain,' Sarah said. 'You can't have any safer place than this in the whole of Dublin. A castle full of soldiers. And besides, they don't shoot at hospitals. Don't you be worrying. The policeman's right. They spread these rumours every time there's someone on a street corner talking about Ireland for the Irish.'

The double doors to the ward kitchen burst open, both at once. Kitty, white-faced and out of breath, sat down on the stool near the door, laid her head on her hands and howled.

'They've killed our policeman. Mr O'Brien. My da's best friend. They've shot him dead. Right at the front gate.'

'Have they taken the castle? The Sinn Feiners? Are they all coming in right now?'

Sarah still had her arm round Mary's shoulder.

'I don't know. I don't know. I ran away as soon as I heard. That might have been my daddy at the gate. Oh, thank goodness my daddy is away fighting in France.'

She was gasping for breath and crying and holding her chest. Sarah took hold of her hand.

'Stay here. Dry your eyes. Look after Mary for me. He may not be dead after all.'

She went out through the long ward. Two nurses in there were trying in vain to get the men to go back into their beds. The crack of the guns and the shouting had got them all at the windows, craning to see what had happened. On the far side of the room away from the windows, one very tall soldier sat on the floor beside his bed, crying quietly and rocking like a child refusing to go back to sleep in case he has a nightmare.

Sarah ran through the next ward and whispered to the sister in charge.

'Is it true the policeman's been shot?'

'Yes. Sh! Don't upset the men.'

'Is he dead?'

'Nobody knows. Go back to your work now. The men must be fed. They'll be wanting their drinks. Just keep them calm.'

By the time Sarah got back to her own ward, the men were back in their beds. No one said anything. There was silence. Only the scraping of knives on plates. The nurses and helpers were meant to have their dinners afterwards but Sarah wasn't hungry. How could anyone eat? How could anyone keep calm when someone they knew might have died? And no one knew what was going to happen next. No one had told them anything. The whole place might be swarming with Sinn Feiners ready to murder them at any moment. But the hospital remained calm.

The sister from the next ward came up to see them in the ward kitchen. Their favourite policeman had had his brains blown out, killed by a single shot. She had gone out to help bring his body in, to see if they could save him, but he had died instantly.

'What about the others?' Kitty's face was red and shining with tears. 'What about the sentries? Were they shot to pieces as well?'

'They managed to get to the guard room.'

'But why didn't they shoot back?' Mary had calmed down enough to be angry. 'Why didn't they defend the castle? That's why they're there. To defend us.'

'The men who were watching from the windows say the sentries have no ammunition. Never do. They say there's no call for it on a normal day.' The sister sighed. 'I don't know. But the Sinn Feiners have gone away.

35

You've nothing to fear. They must have thought better of attacking a hospital.'

She took one of the clean drying cloths down from the pile on the shelf above the sink and held it out to Kitty. 'Now, dry your eyes, young ladies. We may have proper nurse's work to do before the night is out.'

'Excuse me, sister.'

Sarah put her hand up as she always did in class at school. The sister smiled.

'I think my parents will expect me at home for dinner this evening, if there's trouble. But our man won't be coming over to collect me till later this week and I think perhaps I ought to go home now. Will I have to take the tram?'

The sister smiled again.

'They've stopped the trams from running now, my dear. They say the Sinn Feiners have shot the lines to pieces and there's trams lying on their sides.'

Sarah twisted the corner of her starched, white apron, crumpling the edges where her mother's maid had worked so hard to iron and starch them shiny-smooth.

'My parents will wonder where I am.'

'They know where you went to this morning, I hope?'

Sarah nodded and the ward sister shook her head.

'It's a bad business. There's many a family'll be missing sons or daughters tonight, and many with no idea they were sending them off to war when they said goodbye this morning.'

She straightened Sarah's cap, and tucked her black curls in neatly at the sides. 'You'll be safer here in the castle as long as there's shooting going on outside.'

Then she turned away from all of them and reached up to straighten the piles of clean cloths on the shelves, even though they didn't need straightening.

'The government will get this sorted out soon, don't you worry. It'll all be over by morning. I feel sorry for those poor young idiots myself. Those stupid young idiots who've let themselves be taken in by a handful of Sinn Feiners with their nonsense about freedom. It's the Germans we should be fighting for our freedom, not our own countrymen. It can't be right, that shower in the post office setting Irishman against Irishman.'

Then she clapped her hands.

'Let's get the dinner things cleared and the ward tidied now, please. It's a good thing some of us don't have time for thinking about this freedom nonsense.'

Sarah walked around the wards after that, plumping up pillows, picking up books the men had dropped, listening for the single loud reports she thought were rifle shots. The air in the wards was heavy; a fog had dropped down suddenly over the sunshine of that day. The men were quiet, staring at the walls or at books they didn't read, wincing at the distant crackling that Sarah grew to recognize as sniper fire. She wanted to get them all away, even if it were only as far away as her parents' house and garden out in the suburbs, where horses came up to the hedge and the loudest noise was the sound of Mrs Delaney calling to the gardener to bring her some potatoes. She wanted to give them back some peace and quiet, when all she could do was pick their belongings up off the floor. She felt helpless.

That afternoon, she watched as a troop of soldiers arrived and lined up in the barrack yard. She found herself scanning the rows for her brother James, because that would be something good to take with her when this was all over in the morning and she could make her way home to her parents. Nobody knew where the troops were posted. It would be so good to let her parents know that he was not, in fact, being shot at by the Germans in some filthy trench in France but guarding Dublin Castle against a few Irish rebels.

There were plenty of soldiers who reminded her of James, tall and blue-eyed with dark hair. But her brother wasn't among them. The soldiers stood to attention with bayonets fixed, a strong, brave fighting force ready to take on the rebels.

'See, we've nothing to worry about any more,' Kitty whispered. 'Aren't you proud of our men? Will you look at that one over there? Isn't he just a dream?'

Sarah couldn't look at the man of Kitty's dreams. All she could see was her brother and Liam Casey, marching off together the last time she had seen him. She remembered how her mother had said the same thing. 'Aren't you proud of our young men?' And three weeks later Mrs Casey had received the telegram with the news that Liam was dead.

Still, as long as the soldiers stayed inside the barrack yard they were safe enough.

The heavy gates were locked and bolted, keeping the troop of soldiers safe inside the castle they were set to guard. Outside the gates, little boys threw stones at them, trying to lob them over the top, and a tiny girl bent her head down to peep in through the spaces between the iron bars that made up the fence.

Kitty and Sarah leaned out over the window ledge and laughed to the children.

'Go home now,' they shouted. 'Go home.' Then they turned back inside. 'What on earth can their parents be thinking of?'

In the distance, rifles went off like bird-scarers. But from inside the castle it was impossible to see where they were shooting from or who was being hit.

3

The Dublin pavements in Sackville Street and O'Connell Street swirled with smoke, like the kind you see on stage at a pantomime just before the wicked witch appears. Daisy shivered and pulled her dark woollen coat around her. She dipped her hand deep into the pocket on the right side and felt for the revolver someone had taken from a British officer in the GPO.

'They won't be searching women and girls yet,' the sergeant had said. 'Not so long as you're not in uniform.'

There was hardly anything to eat for the Volunteers in the post office, but Daisy wasn't hungry. It was tiredness that nagged at her, tugging her down into nightmares that shook her and punched her awake instead of knocking her out. At first she was relieved to be nudged out of her sleep and ordered to go out into the streets with two women officers searching for food. She had hardly slept at all in the five hour stretch she had been given, in the women's quarters up on the top floor. The shooting from the parapet just outside their windows never stopped. Shooting, and cries of 'Got him!', and screams nearby as Volunteers were hit by British army snipers. Daisy didn't see any of the wounded before they were carried down into the vaults and then somehow taken to Jervis Street hospital for treatment, so she didn't know if Michael was among them. She hadn't seen him since six o'clock the night before when they had last helped to build the barricades together.

Daisy's feet dragged her along. The smoke that swirled

39

around on the pavements covered everything, magical as early morning dew on a meadow by a river.

'That's all the smoke from the shooting.' One of the women was smiling. 'Would you look at that now. You don't notice it in the dark. It's worse than a firework night for smoke.'

It was six o'clock on Tuesday morning and the two women walked quickly, with Daisy in between them.

'If anyone stops us, we're on our way back to your school in Eccles Street—making sure you get back there safely. Isn't that right, Daisy?'

Daisy snapped herself awake.

'But you know I don't want to go back really. I want to stay and fight with you. You won't really make me go back?'

'We've got to have a good reason to be out this early. If not we'll have to use our guns. And we don't want a pitched battle out in the streets. Now you just keep yourself quiet, Daisy, and leave it to us.'

Captain Deirdre Clarke was a teacher for most of the time and a member of the Irish Citizen Army at the weekend.

'What we're looking for is a bread cart. We just do a quiet hold-up, take the cart, and get back to our post. There's men back there waiting on some food. You understand all that, don't you, Daisy? You're just on your way back to school if anyone asks. All right?'

'Yes, captain.'

They were treating her as if she were stupid. She wasn't stupid, just so tired that her brain wasn't working properly.

The minutes swirled by; every second counted out in the regular rat-a-tat of sniper fire. The swirling smoke clutched at the throats of Dublin's streets, cutting off all the air and light. The sun refused to come up. Daisy, walking in between the two taller women, suddenly felt like a prisoner being marched towards execution and she was afraid, so afraid that she started to walk faster than them, as if walking faster would take her beyond the threat of the snipers' bullets. It wasn't that she really wanted to give up and get away from the Volunteers to a place of safety. It wasn't as if she was scared. It was just that she didn't want to get killed right there, with no time to talk to her parents, no time to tell them why she had decided, on the spur of the moment, to join up with the Volunteers and fight for Ireland's freedom. She was sure they would be proud of her, if only she could speak to them and let them know where she was, what she was doing.

Her grandfather had fought for the slaves to be set free. Her mother had fought for women's right to vote. Daisy knew she was only doing what her mother and father would be doing if they were here. All she wanted was the chance to talk to them. She didn't want to get herself killed before she had seen them one more time.

There were no bread carts. The streets were deserted except for a few women. The streets of Dublin belonged to women, scavenging for food or searching for their dead. Around a corner, they came upon two tall women holding on to a handcart, with a little girl standing beside them, all bending over a soldier lying face-down in the gutter.

'Who is he? Is he dead?'

Captain Clarke stepped forward, nudging the body with her foot and rolling the man onto his back. The patch of blood that covered most of the front of his uniform jacket had turned to a purple-black. He was a British soldier.

'He's been dead since yesterday afternoon.'

The older of the two women took hold of his two arms

and motioned to her daughter to lift the soldier by his legs onto the cart. The little girl let go of her mother's hand and stood with her thumb in her mouth, watching them struggle with the corpse.

Daisy felt sick. So this was war. The soldier looked no more than sixteen. His curly red hair was clean and tidy. There wasn't a mark on his face.

'Do you know him? Is he a friend of yours?'

The old woman shook her head, then straightened the soldier's arms out, where they had flopped over the edge of the cart. 'We seen him lying here, out of our window, miss, since yesterday. Whenever the shooting slowed down, I looked out, just to see if anyone had moved him.'

She picked up the handles of the cart while her daughter picked up the tiny girl and turned her face away, burying it in the shoulder of her coat. Three times, the little girl pulled her face out and tried to stare at the soldier's open, staring eyes and each time her mother covered the little girl's eyes and turned her away.

'I wouldn't treat a dog like that. And this is some mother's son. Only a boy, whatever army he belongs to.' The old woman heaved and shoved at the cart until it started to move over the cobbles in the direction of Jervis Street. 'But that's them Sinn Feiners for you. Our brave Irish rebels. Nothing but cowards, the lot of them.'

And she spat as they passed a lamp-post with its copy of the Proclamation pasted up, like the ones Daisy had handed out only the day before to the crowds around the GPO.

A loud report of bullets started up again, but all they could see was smoke. They couldn't see who was firing or who was being fired at.

'Go on. Fire away. Fire away.'

While the old woman struggled and pushed the heavy

cart, the little girl looked back over her mother's shoulder at Daisy and kept staring at her for as long as she could, as Daisy watched the miserable little funeral procession disappear into the smoke.

Captain Clarke patted her on the shoulders. 'Come on, lassie. We have soldiers to feed.'

It was six-thirty. Daisy strained to listen. The streets were suddenly quiet again. She was tired. She realized she had a headache from being alert to every sound; from life being ruled by the rhythm, second-by-second, of rifles firing.

So this was war.

And now the streets were as quiet as they were on holy days at six when Sister Mary marched them off to mass at the cathedral and the girls were told not to talk. Daisy tried to sense where the next load of bullets would come from. Told herself not to be afraid. Told herself she had a gun and she could use it if she needed to. But in the quiet, empty streets there was no one to shoot at, only invisible hands firing at them, invisible eyes watching them from out of the swirling darkness.

Daisy kept herself awake and kept herself moving by trying to use her thoughts to take herself back. Back to the time before she had seen a young man dead in the road. Back to the boredom of walking in crocodiles to mass with Sister Mary. She tried to shut out the young soldier and go back to the time her grandfather had taught her to shoot out on Rhode Island, first at targets on a tree and then at the moving discs he threw into the air. He'd told everyone what a good shot she was. He said he'd never seen a girl who could shoot that well and promised he'd take her with him the first time he went hunting after she was fourteen.

And then her father had been moved over to Europe

and her mother and father had decided to send her to school in the convent.

The streets were quiet. They were walking too far away from the GPO, and in the wrong direction for Eccles Street. No one would believe their story about getting Daisy safely back to school if they were stopped. But they needed food for the troops.

It was quite simple, the job they had to do. Plenty of others had managed it before them. The whole of the previous day, women Volunteers had gone out with revolvers, stopping cars and carts with provisions. There was very little resistance. All you did was to say to the driver, 'I am commandeering this cart in the name of the Irish Republican Army.' That was the way they had managed to get food round to all the troops stationed in the city. But the city was silent now and not in the mood to be generous. There was no sign of a bread cart.

They turned back, taking a different route, none of them saying out loud the words that were going round their heads. If they don't manage to shoot us out of the GPO, they'll starve us out. They walked quickly, the leather soles on their shoes tap-tapping on the cobbles.

'Why haven't we seen any British soldiers yet?' Daisy whispered, trying not to break the silence. 'Why is it so quiet? Why haven't they started fighting us properly yet?'

At every street corner there were IRA barricades, house or shop windows broken and mattresses stuffed inside for protection. There were barricades made of burnt-out carts and cars. There were walls collapsed and deserted, boarded-up buildings. But nowhere was there evidence of the British army. Daisy couldn't understand it. On any normal day in Dublin, in cafés, on street corners, you would see men in British army uniform strolling round as if they owned the place. Where had they all gone now?

The two women on either side of her walked on, mo[re]
quickly and in silence until Captain Clarke said, 'They've
plenty of snipers about. But you're right. There's not
enough. They're saving their fire. They're re-grouping.
They'll start to attack us when they're strong enough.'

Ahead of them they saw thick, black smoke from a
building burning several streets away and then suddenly,
round the corner, a group of soldiers on horseback came
riding, slowly, not more than five or six of them.

'Keep calm. Keep looking straight ahead. Let me talk.'

The three women moved onto the narrow pavement
while the horses rode along down the centre of the
street.

'Are they British? Or are they ours?'

Daisy had her hand in her pocket, clutching her
revolver, but still she was half asleep and half paralysed
with fear.

Captain Clarke smiled. 'And where would we get
beautiful horses like that?' She nodded at the first lancer
on horseback. 'A very good morning to you, officer.'

'Not a good morning, ma'am, for three ladies like
you to be out on the streets. It's not safe for anyone at
the moment. I would advise you to get yourselves to a
place of safety without delay.'

'That's where we're heading, officer. I'm taking this
young lady back to her school in Eccles Street. She was
separated from her friends yesterday and the nuns will be
sick with worry. They haven't been doing much shooting
yet. That's why we ventured out.'

The officer touched his cap. 'Just get there as fast as
you can, ma'am. And can I urge you, when you get
yourselves safe inside the convent stay there until all this
is over. We've got the measure of the rebels. It shouldn't
be too long now.'

Then all the lancers saluted and rode on past them.

ook back.' Captain Clarke moved them along
r. 'Don't show your feelings. Don't, whatever
look relieved. There may be British soldiers
out of windows now. There may be snipers
e ignored us because we're not in uniform.
Remember who we're supposed to be. Just keep
moving.'

Behind them there was a burst of firing.

'Don't look back. Keep moving.'

'But who is firing?' said Daisy. 'Is it one of ours or
one of theirs?'

'I don't know,' Captain Clarke shouted and pushed
them sideways into a shop doorway. 'Get down. How
should I know who's firing? Do you think I have eyes in
the back of my head?'

From the shelter of the shop doorway, Daisy looked
back up the street, the way they had come. Another
building had been set on fire, a bicycle shop, and thick,
black smoke from the burning tyres wrapped its way like
an awful picture frame around everything that Daisy saw
next. Bullets were still firing, rasping and biting like an
angry old dog. It looked as if nothing would ever stop
their savage firing. Then through the frame of thick, black
smoke Daisy saw the first picture, an image she would
never forget. Horses and riders, the beautiful, black horses
and the British soldiers who had saluted them and told
them to be careful two minutes before were one,
struggling, jerking mass, their limbs forced to dance to
the rhythm of bullets still firing.

Then the noise of the shooting stopped. There was
silence. Another burst of firing. Then a longer silence.
Daisy couldn't cry. She squeezed her fist hard into her
mouth. Captain Clarke put an arm on her shoulder.

'Stay down. Don't move.'

There was absolute silence. Then one of the horses

pulled itself out from under the weight of its fallen rider and managed to stand.

'She's not hurt.' The words came mangled from Daisy's clamped-up mouth.

'That's a good girl, Daisy. Stay where you are. Keep calm.'

They watched the horse pushing her nose against the body of her rider. Daisy started to stand up, wanting to run from the shelter of the shop doorway and lead the horse to safety, but the two other women took her by the shoulders and held her down.

'It's not safe. No movement. Keep down.'

A single shot rang out and the horse fell dead, collapsing over her master.

No one spoke. In the shop doorway, they crouched for what seemed like an age, but was probably only ten minutes. Then, with no more shooting at the end of the street, they slowly moved on. It was ten o'clock and still there was no sign of food. Daisy didn't want to move on any more. Her holiday shoes pinched at her toes and her coat was getting too hot to wear, but she wasn't allowed to take it off. The hat they had made her wear tightened over the crown of her head because they had made her do what she never did, coil her blonde plaits around her head and stick hairpins in to make the plaits stay out of sight.

'You'll be a sitting target in that bright, white dress and with your hair so fair,' they said. 'There's no one round here with hair like that.'

Daisy wanted to rip the small neat hat off her head and let her plaits hang down over her shoulders. She was suffocating in the heat from the sun and the burning buildings and the firing of bullets everywhere.

'Please can I take my coat off, Deirdre?' She trotted along behind the two women now, like a disgruntled toddler.

'You must call me Captain Clarke. You're in the army now. On active service. You have to follow orders, and I say if you take your coat off you make us all sitting targets. It's dangerous to be out here. We've got to keep moving.'

Dublin still didn't look dangerous. Not at the times when the snipers stopped firing. A strange mixture of people filled some of the streets, women pushing prams for all the world as if they were taking the baby out for a breath of fresh air until you saw that the prams were full of clothes or shoes looted from broken shop-windows. Sometimes they came across priests running around telling people to get themselves home. In other places, they found themselves dashing from doorway to doorway, the emptiness and silence in that street being the only clue there was that a sniper was at work. They never knew whose side the firing came from, only trusting to luck to help them escape being fired on themselves.

After the group of soldiers on horseback they didn't see another soul in uniform. There were no soldiers, no firemen, no policemen. The fires that were started were just left to burn, and the looters soon learned that no policeman in uniform was going to turn out to stop them. There was firing going on all around them in the centre of the city, but the looters, staggering with their loads of alcohol and jewellery, didn't seem to care about the danger.

On one street corner, a boy was standing in the broken window of a hat shop, juggling summer straw hats and pitching them out into the waiting crowd. Noblett's sweet shop was raided by dozens of little boys and girls. Their mothers reached in to the broken windows of jeweller's shops and pulled their hands out with rings on every finger. Poor children helped themselves to toys, and poor men and women helped themselves to too much beer and wine. It was like watching people on holiday, enjoying themselves at the fair. But there was no food to be had, anywhere.

At midday they trudged back up to the entrance to the GPO. While they were away, the men had rolled out sheets of barbed wire in front of the barricades, eight feet high.

'In case they try a cavalry attack at night.' Captain Clarke nodded. 'They've got to think of everything.'

Daisy winced, remembering the dead and dying men and horses framed by thick black smoke. But she didn't say anything. No one was going to see her cry.

Inside, in the basement of the GPO, other groups had been more successful at finding food than they had. There were sacks and sacks of oats down there and a huge pot of hot porridge was ready for anyone coming back from outside duty. Daisy pulled her horrible hat off and pulled all the hairpins out, one by one, so that her plaits cascaded down her back. She rubbed at her aching head where the hairpins had stuck in and then at her aching, blistered feet, where her Sunday shoes had pinched on the long march through the city. She wasn't dressed to go to war. She took her coat off, laid it down on the stone floor of the basement, and slumped back against one of the pillars.

It was noisy in the basement, with Volunteers coming and going and queuing up to be fed. All around her, men and women were talking about their experiences and calling out greetings to friends. But the sound of the bullets had gone, drowned by the weight of the building above them. She fell asleep.

It was Michael who woke her at five o'clock and made her eat a bowl of porridge and drink a cup of tea. He had spent the day with a detachment making bombs and filling shotgun cartridges.

'There was no fighting,' he said. 'Maybe there won't

be any fighting. Maybe the British will give in without a fight, because they know we're right. Maybe we won't have to use the guns and bombs. They say we've had no serious casualties so far. No one dead. The longer we hold out here, the better our chances of taking Ireland for the Irish.'

Daisy leaned back against the stone pillar, sipping her tea slowly like an invalid recovering from a long illness. She wanted to shout at Michael, to tell him he was stupid if he believed all those stories about no serious casualties, but she felt weak and sick, too sick to eat and almost too sick to talk.

'There was fighting,' she spoke very quietly. 'We saw British soldiers dead. And horses. They were shooting the horses as well. They're not telling you the truth.'

He wasn't going to see her cry. No one was going to see her cry. It wasn't right to cry about a horse, when people were getting themselves killed all around. But it was the horse being killed after all the soldiers were already dead. That was what had got to her and made her want to cry. She frowned. What did Michael know about anything, talking as if no one was getting killed? How old was he anyway? Just a stupid boy who'd got himself tied up in something he knew nothing about. Oh, he'd heard all the talk about Ireland and wanting the British out of Ireland, but what did he know of the price to be paid? When had he ever seen a young soldier thrown on a handcart like any old sack of potatoes or flour and dragged away?

'There's going to be fighting here, Michael. We're all going to be killed. You know that, don't you?'

Michael scraped the last of his porridge out of the bowl and licked it clean.

'That's what I joined up with the Volunteers for. To die for my country. I'm not afraid.'

Tuesday night was quiet. So quiet that Daisy slept until early the next morning. They had time to prepare for the attack that was bound to come, stacking up piles of ammunition at all the firing posts, before suddenly the sniping became much more intense. Volunteers in the shops and houses all around them had already started firing out at the British troops as they were being brought into position. But Daisy and Michael were in the best place after all. The GPO was still safe, so safe that the generals decided to move troops out from there to other posts to help them with reinforcements.

Michael was one of the soldiers who volunteered to be moved out to Abbey Street. After two days of careful preparations to defend the post office he thought he wasn't afraid any more. The shooting had all taken place in the darkness, shooting by people he couldn't see, with the cries, sometimes, of invisible victims. He wanted to see more action. He didn't care if he got killed, like his brother out in France. And if he didn't get himself killed, well then, when this was all over, he wanted to talk about what he had done for Ireland, not about how he had waited quietly in the GPO for the British to give in. He had heard the men at the Volunteer meetings talk about how they had waited long enough to see some action. He had lied about his age so they would let him join them. He wasn't going to hide away in the basement of the GPO when it was almost as safe there as if he was back home in his own bed.

There had been no sniping near to where they were since the first few hours when they took the GPO. It was obvious to everyone who had been in the post office from the beginning that all the opposition had been taken out. General Connolly himself talked to them about the important job there was for them in Abbey Street, defending the new republic's radio communications. The advance party was already there. The general marched out with them in groups and left them at the corner of O'Connell Street and then came back to direct each of the following groups as they came. Michael, in the last group, marched out without a hat. He told the sergeant he didn't have one, that he'd never had a hat, but the sergeant sent him back, telling him he might be allowed to catch up with the group if he got himself properly dressed.

When Michael rushed back out, a borrowed hat on his head, there was no sign of anyone, neither the general nor the men. He hesitated. He knew which way they had gone, but he wasn't sure if he had permission to follow them.

He edged his way slowly to the corner of O'Connell Street and Lower Abbey Street, just as the noise of firing stopped. Both streets looked empty. The smoke from the shooting grabbed at his throat. He moved slowly down the left-hand side of Abbey Street. It was getting dark, but it was light enough for him to see the huge barricade the Volunteers had built across the street. They had everything piled on it, bicycles, big rolls of paper from a paper store, even an armchair.

But it was all too quiet. There was no way of telling which shops or houses would give shelter to one of the rebels, which ones were already occupied by the British army, not when it was as quiet as the grave and turning dark. Michael decided to turn back and get himself into the post office until the next morning. He had stepped back for cover into a shop doorway just in time when the shooting started again. He was forced to dodge into the next shop doorway, and the next. Running and hiding, running and hiding. It didn't look as if anyone was shooting at him directly, but it was so dark now that whoever was shooting would have been happy whatever they hit.

Michael settled into a shop doorway just past the corner into O'Connell Street, to catch his breath again before making another dash towards the post office. As he sat down his hand touched the leather of a soldier's boot instead of a stone step. He moved his hands. The whole of the step was wet with blood. There was a dead soldier half-propped against the wall, a man with a peaked cap, an officer in the uniform of a Volunteer, legs stretched out, eyes closed.

Michael leaned against the wall and closed his eyes too. He knew that if he moved he would be sick, but he knew he had to stay calm. People were going to die. He was going to see death. He had to learn to see death. He crawled closer and the man opened his eyes and whispered, 'How long have you been there?' And closed his eyes again, as if he was worn out by that one question.

'I've just taken cover here, sir. Excuse me, sir. How long have *you* been here?'

The officer pointed to his watch and then closed his eyes again. 'It feels a long, long time, but I think it's ten minutes since he got me.' He pointed to one of his legs. 'The bone's all shot up. I've crawled back to here.'

It was too dark to see what had happened. Michael wiped his hands, soaked with the man's blood, on to his own trousers and then sprang out of the doorway, making a run for it to the GPO.

By the time Michael got back to the shop door with the stretcher party, the officer was completely unconscious from loss of blood. They carried him back to the GPO, half running, half crawling through the darkness.

4

So this is war. There was no time to say the words to the nurses running past and only slowing to a walk when one of the ward sisters appeared. There was no time to write the words down. Sarah had the idea she ought to write about what was happening, a letter to her parents or even a diary. She ought to let someone know about it, but there was no time.

So this is war. There was no time, and no reason, for Sarah to say the words going round in her head to the men all around her. The injured men who'd been in the castle for a few weeks, recovering from their time in France, were out of their beds now when they shouldn't be, doing whatever they could to help the rushing, hurrying nurses. The number of men who'd been wounded that afternoon was far greater than the number in Sarah's ward. But there was no point in repeating the words to them. So this is war. They had been to war and come back. They knew what war looked like.

What Sarah saw was war. The room outside the supper kitchen, the corridors all along from one stairway to the next, were painted with blood, with men laid out on waterproof sheets or mackintoshes the colour of blood. Pain shrieked from mangled legs and faces even when the wounded soldiers lay in silence, too shocked to make a sound. The words marched round in Sarah's head and stayed there marching up and down, up and down, because there was no one to say the words to.

So this is war.

The room opposite the supper kitchen had been turned into an operating theatre. The castle hospital was filled with three times as many men as usual, but extra doctors and nurses couldn't get through. People were rushing around with fierce, calm masks on their faces, doing what had to be done. They tried to keep the doors closed on the room where two doctors were working as fast as they could to patch up the broken men, but so much was happening, so much was needed. The doors to the operating theatre flew open yet again.

The matron stopped and looked into Sarah's face. 'You're not one of my nurses, are you, child?'

Sarah shook her head. 'I'm a helper, ma'am. I couldn't get home last night.'

'Then you're very good at making tea, no doubt.'

Sarah nodded.

'Now dry your eyes. No, not with those hands.'

The matron held out a clean handkerchief and dabbed at Sarah's eyes herself. Then she turned her round by her shoulders and took her into the supper kitchen to wash the blood off her hands. She stood over Sarah, her voice unravelling threads of calm from the great knot of chaos outside the small room.

'Use plenty of soap, mind. You always have to scrub up clean in a hospital.'

Then she steered Sarah past the row of waiting men in the corridor. Some of the injured men were lying quietly, eyes closed or eyes staring in pain far away to the high ceiling. Some were screaming. Some had their faces covered to conceal a gaping wound. All of them cried out for attention, for someone to take them and make them better. Matron steered Sarah briskly along the row until they got to the bottom of the stairs. Then she saw that they wouldn't be allowed to go down the usual way and across the yard to the main section of the hospital.

'It's too dangerous to cross the yard at the moment. The rebels are still firing on the castle from every which way. We'll want to get you home safely to your mother when all of this is over.'

They had to take a detour through the old throne room, so that by the time they reached the sterilizing room next to the convalescent wards they were in another world, a world where everything was as it should be in a hospital, clean and white, calm and quiet.

Left alone, Sarah felt ashamed of herself for letting anyone see she was upset, when she had so little reason to be. She was old enough to be working as a nurse— nearly fourteen. She knew that most girls of her age were out at work by then. And if she was old enough to work as a nurse, she was old enough to cope with what it meant to be a nurse even in a war. She looked around to see whether anyone was watching from the corridor outside and then put her head down on the table and wept.

The pots and kettles steaming all around her, with their lids dancing around and the water overflowing and spitting onto the range, teased her out of her crying. Sarah gave herself a good shake and remembered why she was there—to get the men the cup of tea they needed. At the same time, the peace was shattered again as bullets flew past the sterilizing room window and smashed into the wall across the yard. Sarah pulled a stool up to the sink near the window and climbed on it, but she was so small that she still couldn't see out. Then she started to climb onto the draining board, to see if she could find out what was happening, who was shooting outside the high window.

'Are you a lunatic, or what?'

Kitty had grabbed her by the ankle.

'Will you get down from there this minute. Don't you

know them idiots are firing at every window they can see people at? They don't stop to ask are you a soldier or someone's old granny just taking a breath of fresh air. Them Sinn Feiners are spraying the world with bullets just like my grandpa would be sowing seed in one of his fields.' And she spread her arms out and made as if to scatter seed all around her over a field that stretched as far as the eye could see. 'I thought you were clever enough to be at one of those grand English schools. Don't you want to go back to school? Are you really such an idiot? Do you really want to get yourself killed?'

Sarah shook her head.

'Then get yourself down off that stool right now. And come and help me with the tea. The upstairs men are playing up like you wouldn't believe it.'

'What are they doing?'

Sarah started to set out the white teacups in rows on the linen cloth they always laid out on top of the trolley.

'Ach. They're like children.' Kitty put four white bowls of sugar down on the second shelf of the trolley. Then she laughed. 'The milkman got through this lunchtime. Our little man pushing his little cart brought us the hospital milk through all them crazy Sinn Feiners as cool as if there was nothing happening.' She lifted a huge pan of milk, half the size of herself, down onto the floor where she could reach into it better, and ladled it out into jugs.

'Mind you, he only brought enough milk for normal teas. He didn't reckon on all the extra men we've got at the moment. If he gets through to us tomorrow, he'll be needing to bring twice as much.'

Sarah helped her to heave the great churn of milk back onto the draining board.

'What did you say the men were up to? The men upstairs. Did matron have to shout at them?'

'Ach, matron's nowhere to be seen. Doesn't she have enough to do with all those poor, half-dead creatures being trailed in downstairs? And there's no more nurses can get through with all this shooting going on. She's left us alone with the ones up here.' Kitty laughed again. 'It's up to us to make sure they behave themselves.'

The trolley's wheels squeaked out a protest at the weight it was carrying and it swerved from side to side as they both pushed it towards the ward. Sarah walked on ahead and pushed open the swing door so Kitty could help the trolley through. Then she stopped, stepped back, and let the doors swing shut behind her. She shook her head at Kitty.

'We can't give them their tea. They're all out of bed. All over the place. What would matron say? We can't serve the tea unless they're all sitting quietly in their beds. That's where they're all supposed to be. What are they thinking of?'

Kitty pursed her lips and shook her head.

'They're like my sister's children. They've all just got too excited.'

Then she walked into the ward, with Sarah behind her.

Most of the men were at one of the windows, some in their dressing gowns, some just in pyjamas. Some were sitting on the edge of their beds. The only one still in bed was a sergeant who couldn't sit up until they had propped him up with four pillows. Kitty stood with her hands on her hips. She turned to Sarah.

'Well, there's no point in wearing me voice-box out. They wouldn't listen to me anyway. That would be a waste of time.'

So she just stood there. Hands on hips. One or two of the men turned round from the window.

'Hey up! Sister's annoyed, lads.'

A tall, lanky young soldier with a moustache hobbled away from the window on his crutches.

'You won't get no tea if you're not back in bed, lads,' he shouted and let himself down gently into the chair next to his bed.

Kitty smiled, then shook her head and pointed slowly, from his chair over on to his bed. He got the message and heaved himself onto the bed. Then other men slowly calmed down and gradually got themselves back to where they should be.

Only one of the soldiers was still out of bed, not noticing what had happened, paying no attention to Kitty or all the other men. He was sitting on the floor clinging to the leg of the bed, the tall young soldier making himself as small as possible, his face white with horror. Sarah went over to him and sat beside him.

'Won't you get back into your bed now? You'll be getting cold here on the floor. And your leg will never get better unless you rest it stretched out in bed.'

After a long time the young man looked at her. His blue eyes were veined with red from lack of sleep and his face was drawn tight like a thin mask over the bones. She thought he could be sixteen, but fear had turned him into a sixty year old.

'We're in hell again, nurse. The Germans are coming back to get us. None of us are safe. Not here.'

He closed his eyes tightly and groaned as another hail of bullets whizzed past the window where the men had just been fighting each other to get the best look-out place.

'I thought it was all over, but we're in hell again.'

He put out his right hand as if to help himself stand up, but he didn't have the strength. 'We might as well go back to France, nurse, if the Germans are coming here to get us.'

The soldier next to him got out of bed and leaned over the boy on the floor. 'He lost his mate under heavy shelling, I've heard. He's not that old either.' He stroked the boy on the head as you would do with a frightened child. 'He wasn't that badly hurt. But his best mate were dead in the trenches next to him for ten hours under fire and they couldn't do owt. They couldn't move the dead 'un. None of the others could move away from him.'

He nodded in the direction of the open window the men had all been fighting to look out of. 'That's just sniping,' he said. 'Someone with a rifle taking pot-shots at us, like you shoot rabbits when they bolt across a field.' Then he grabbed at Sarah's sleeve. 'Listen to that.'

Sarah didn't know what she was listening for in the noise of bullets whistling and stone cracking and heavy trucks and ambulances pulling up in the yard of the castle.

'No, listen. Not the bullets. Further away. It's still far away. Can't you hear them shelling?'

He held on to her sleeve like someone holding on to the only handrail over a very steep drop. 'There it is. Listen. Thud. Boom. Quiet. Now everything's quiet again. And there it is again. Thud. Boom. Quiet. And another ten poor sods are dead and gone. Thud. Boom!' He started to slowly clap his hands as the rhythm of the shells became clearer and then stopped at a break in the shelling.

The soldier on the floor had his hands over his ears and was crying quietly.

'You stand a chance with a sniper,' the second soldier said. 'But not when they start shelling and a shell lands right on your trench. And if you survive and everyone around you's been blown to pieces . . . '

He nodded at the soldier crouched on the floor. Then he stood up and helped Kitty and Sarah to half lift, half drag the tall young man and lie him down on his bed. After a while, he stopped crying and lay there quietly, on his side, staring at the wall.

Sarah climbed up onto a chair again and without thinking leaned out to grab the window handle and shut the window. She paused as she saw the rows of new troops arriving and lining up in the yard below. How many of those would be lying in the hospital, or lying dead in a Dublin street, the next day?

'Again? Are you a lunatic, or what?' Kitty had finally decided to raise her voice. 'Will you come down from that window and stop trying to get yourself killed.'

There was a cheer as Sarah stepped down from the chair.

'Now,' Kitty stood at the entrance to the ward, 'have you all decided to behave yourselves now? Do you want your cup of tea or don't you?'

There was another loud cheer as the two nurses went outside to get the tea trolley.

'How did you do that?' Sarah moved to hold open the doors.

'What?'

'How did you make them all get back into bed and be quiet?'

'Ach. They're all like children. Like my brothers and sisters. You've not got to shout, that's all. If you shout, they don't listen to you.'

'Yes, but you didn't say anything.'

'Ah, but they knew I wanted them to be quiet and get back into bed or they wouldn't get their tea.'

'How? How did they know all that?'

Kitty smiled and shrugged her shoulders and pushed the heavy trolley through the doors. There was the beginning of a loud cheer again and she stopped, halfway in and half out of the door until the noise subsided. Then two of the soldiers who were able to move around easily hopped out of bed again and volunteered to serve the others. Soon the atmosphere was calm enough for Sarah and Kitty to take temperatures, write on the charts at the ends of the beds, and clear away the tea things.

'You'd almost think that all those terrible things downstairs weren't happening any longer,' Sarah said, as if words could bring back the normality of the morning before. But she couldn't forget the rows of the injured lying in the corridors, the noise of men screaming in pain, and the sight of the nurses and doctors calmly, quietly going through the row of incoming patients, picking out from the crowd of injured men the ones who needed to be operated on immediately, leaving for an hour or two the ones who could be left.

There was no going home that second day either and no way of anyone getting news through to relatives. Sarah's parents knew she was in the castle, and the castle had not been taken by the rebels yet, and that would have to do.

The matron came to their ward later on in the evening, leaving an older nurse in charge. 'The two of you need to get some sleep,' she said, and led them yet another strange route along the inside courtyard balconies and through underground corridors in the castle to where there were other nurses trying to sleep. From the landing overlooking the inside courtyard they could see soldiers warming their hands at two large watch-fires lighting up the darkness. The only other points of light were flashes of red and white, quick bursts like fireworks, shooting up into the dark sky.

Sarah was so exhausted she fell asleep immediately. But nobody slept for long in that week. After only an hour or two she was shaken awake.

'Get up, Sarah. We'll have to move. The rebels are firing at our windows.'

Kitty's hair hung loose down her back, not even in the neat pigtails she usually wore to make her hair curl while she was asleep. Sarah scooped her long, heavy hair into her hand and tied it into a thick knot at the back.

'Here, you can borrow my dressing gown. We've got to move quickly. Grab hold of your uniform. We'll need to get dressed over the other side. Quickly. They're shooting directly at that window.' Sarah threw on her coat over her nightdress, grabbed at the pile of clothes she had remembered to fold only an hour or two before as they collapsed into bed and followed Kitty out into the dark corridor. The air was quiet again. The corridor was pitch dark. Sarah wanted to stop right where she was, put down her bundle of clothes, and lie down and go to sleep again. Why couldn't they go to sleep right there? She didn't want to keep moving, didn't want to keep on fighting the tiredness.

She slumped down with her back to the wall and sat on the floor. They were the last out of the room.

'I'm tired, Kitty. Can't we just stop here? There's nobody around.'

'Don't you know anything?'

Kitty, her arms round her own bundle of clothes, tugged at Sarah's collar.

'This is the way they bring the injured men in to the receiving area, from the yard door down there. We can't just stop here. We've got to get back to the nurse's quarters.'

'But they moved us out of there last night because of the sniper.'

'They've taken him out. It's not dangerous there any more. Now come on. Get moving.'

Sarah pulled herself up again. She had no idea of time any more. The war had started at lunchtime, just as they were serving out lunch for the men. Only a day and a half had gone by and yet it was half a lifetime. What did her brother feel, what did all the men feel, out in France for months and months of noise and death?

The corridors were dark and cool and quiet, with only an oil lamp burning on the landing. She wanted to sleep. It was half-past one when they reached the nurses' quarters, found themselves a bed, and fell asleep.

5

Wherever Michael turned, arrows of fire, red and yellow flames, shot at him out of a hole of blackness and then fell to earth, like a marvellous firework display. He didn't know where to begin shooting back. He had thought it would be easy, picking up a gun, taking aim and firing. He watched when other people were on lookout. They fired whenever sniping was directed at them, from the rooftops or from the windows of houses they hadn't managed to capture around the GPO. They kept on firing until the shout went up, 'You've taken him out now. It's all over.' You never saw the person on the other side. You never saw who you were shooting at, only the damage they'd done and the blessed silence when they were gone.

'That's where it's coming from,' said Michael.

He leaned forward, took aim and fired. The Mauser rifle kicked up towards his face whenever he pulled the trigger.

'Shove the gun in tighter to your shoulder next time.' Daisy grabbed the rifle off him and showed him again how to hold it. 'It'll leave a bruise on your shoulder. They always do. But it's better than getting it in your face.'

Michael fired again and heard the bullets clang off the metal lamp-posts outside, somewhere to his left. This time his shoulder took the full force of the rifle kicking back at him, battering him so that he wanted to cry out in pain. And all for nothing. The invisible enemies carried on shooting at their position up on the roof, sending out over and over again their bright shooting stars to burst open the darkness.

Michael was frightened of his fear. In all the weeks leading up to Easter Sunday evening, when they were finally given their orders to get themselves into the city and then get together in twos and threes, Michael had never been afraid. Everyone talked then of how good it was to be a soldier. Everyone he knew had been talking about it for as long as he could remember. His friends had talked about volunteering to go out and fight in France, even though they were too young. His brother, Diarmid, had volunteered without telling his parents, months before he was old enough, and had lied about his age so he could sign up. Diarmid had shown no sign of being afraid on that one time he had been home for a visit. He hadn't said a word about shooting and bloodshed and the wounded screaming for help. But that was the last they had heard from him.

Michael had always known that if ever he went out to fight it was Ireland he would fight for, his own country. It wasn't that he was afraid of the Germans out in France. It was just that the English war with the Germans had nothing to do with him. He had proved he wasn't afraid when he volunteered for the Irish Republican Army. He had spent those last few months parading and meeting in secret and now it was all out in the open. He was firing real bullets, spraying the Dublin streets in a storm of fire. And he was afraid.

'That's right,' Daisy said. 'Don't keep firing all the time. Let them think they've taken us out. Then they'll be off their guard.'

Their relief arrived and Daisy put her rifle down and moved right to the back of the building. Michael followed her to where there was a small amount of light from one of the oil lamps. They both slumped down on the floor with their backs to the wall and Michael watched as she took a black-backed book with a red leather spine out of her coat pocket.

'I always write something. At the end of every day.' She pulled a face when she saw him looking at her. 'It's just so I remember all I wanted to tell my mother and father when I see them again.' She held up the book. 'If they shoot me before they get you, you'll have to make sure my parents get this, so they know what happened. But you're not to read it. All right?' Michael nodded.

Her pencil was broken and she borrowed Michael's knife to sharpen it. When Daisy had finished writing, she snapped the diary shut.

'I put you in there today.'

'What? For lending you my knife to sharpen your pencil?'

'For being a hero with the general. Helping them to get him back in under fire when the shooting had smashed up his leg so he couldn't walk. That makes you a hero.'

Michael frowned. 'I couldn't have just left him, could I?'

Daisy stood up, put her diary into her deep coat pockets, and rolled up the coat. The hair had straggled out of her tightly bound plaits so that strands of hair were sticking out all over the place; her bright, white dress was crumpled and filthy from the soot and the smoke and from sleeping on the ground.

'Come on, don't just sit there looking glum,' she said. 'It's not going to get better by sitting here with a long face. We need to eat.'

Down in the cellar, the corner where they queued up for something to eat had been taken over by Volunteers with red-cross armbands dashing backwards and forwards asking for boiling water. It was no longer possible to get the wounded out under cover and take them to hospitals

67

to get them out of danger. All the wounded had to be treated by the one doctor they had with them. And that afternoon the shelling had begun. People had even started to get used to the sounds. There would be a loud thud, then an explosion and a whole building with everyone inside it was blown apart. But the shelling was still not close enough to the GPO to threaten the Volunteers who were lucky to be inside.

They heard that the Dublin fire brigade was out of action. None of the fire-fighters had been out on the streets since the first day of fighting. At first, the rebels had shot at anyone in uniform, and policemen and firemen as well as soldiers had been ordered to take cover. So the fires that were ignited by the shelling burned away unchecked. Flames like savage jungle cats leaped from one building to another across the Dublin streets or burned their way through the barricades the rebels had set up from commandeered cars and carts and piles of furniture.

Daisy and Michael took their porridge and climbed the stone stairs right up to the top of the building. All the shooting was concentrated on the Henry Street side of the GPO and the front, where the rebels had planted their two flags, was empty.

'I know how we can get out onto the roof, on the parapet where all the statues are.' Michael found the metal door easily, even in the dark.

'Keep down,' Daisy said. 'Are you crazy? You'll be a clear target up there, like the statues standing out against the roof line.'

But Michael didn't care. It was quiet out there on the roof. He wanted to get out into the fresh air. He wanted to be free of the fear of getting wounded that grabbed at him and threatened to make him sick whenever he walked down into the basement and saw the rows of wounded

Volunteers, men and women, sitting there or lying screaming on the ground, waiting to be treated. He'd had enough of being afraid. He wanted to get himself killed if that was what was going to happen anyway, to die for Ireland in a mad, glorious rush instead of hiding in cellars and dark corridors. Wasn't that the reason they were fighting in the first place? To die for their country? He crept slowly along the parapet and then stood up next to one of the statues, dead still, arms held out in imitation of the next statue along.

'Michael, will you get yourself back in here this minute!' Daisy crouched by the door. 'We've managed to hold out in this place for three days now without getting ourselves killed. Now come back in. Do you hear me? This minute. You don't have to be killed tonight. You don't have to be killed at all if you can help it. Will you come back in here? We've a job to do and it's not over yet.'

Michael stood there, like a statue, among the statues over the portico, and gazed at the Dublin sky. From up on high he saw the acres of flames and red-hot buildings, as if a volcano somewhere up above and outside the city had erupted and was pouring out its burning lava. The tap-tap-tap of quick firing guns was joined now by the crashing of bombs and shells and the cracking and groaning as great buildings collapsed. In the darkness, the firing, the fires were still beautiful, flaming out against the night sky. They had held out against the might of the British army for three days and had the will to fight to the death if that was what had to happen. Michael felt proud and excited. For that moment he wasn't afraid. Was this what they meant when they talked of freedom?

Slowly he edged his way back to the metal door in the roof, not bothering to crouch down or try to hide.

'You're mad,' Daisy said. Then she stood up and shook her crumpled clothes. 'They're calling for help. They want us down there to help with the wounded.'

That was when Michael's fear came back again, fear like deep claws ripping into his stomach, fear like a drug, taking away all sensation, all movement apart from the rushing waves of fear twisting and grappling at his arms and legs, fear taking him prisoner.

Walking among the wounded, helping with dressings, holding them down while they screamed with pain because there was no morphine in the GPO, was the other face of freedom. Three days of constant firing and no time for food and fires all around them, the whole of Dublin drowning in flames. Michael closed his eyes and clenched his teeth together while he stood beside a stretcher holding out a bowl of hot water for one of the medical officers. Three days of people being shot and wounded and killed. Long nights of people screaming out in pain. How long had his brother been out in France? Five months? Six months?

He had lost track of the time his brother had been away. All he knew was the black hole between the time before Diarmid disappeared and went off to join the British army and the time afterwards, now he was gone and no one knew where he was. He had disappeared early one morning. An ordinary day, the same as all the other mornings when Michael and his brother helped their father with the milking before they went off to school. Their mother was waiting with a good breakfast as she always did, and Michael and his father had had to go inside and tell her that Diarmid was gone.

Afterwards, after Diarmid's only visit home, their mother had disappeared into herself, cooking and cleaning and then sitting alone near the fire staring at her memories of her lost son. Michael thought of his mother staring into the fire all the time he was sitting beside the stretcher with a kettle of water in his left hand. He held his other hand pressed over the eyes of a Volunteer who was going to have to lose her leg. He blocked out all the screaming and all the pain in silent wounded faces by dreaming of his mother and how he would help her face the future. If he got out of there alive, he would go looking for Diarmid, would find out what had happened to him and bring him home.

'Are you asleep or what?'

The young woman with the red-cross armband snapped at him and shook him out of his thoughts. 'If you're going to help with boiling hot water, you might stay awake,' she said. 'Being scalded is not what she needs on top of the mess they've made of her leg.'

6

Like a pattern on an ancient vase the soldiers lined up closely in rows out in the darkened yard. Not real people. Not men and boys with jobs and families waiting for them back home. Not men and boys who joked and sang and swore. But a row of zigzag lines, a pattern made by the bayonets held at the same angle flashing in the dark. A pattern of silhouetted shapes. There was no colour in the dark. Not a man with black hair here, a sandy-haired boy there. But a pattern of heads in profile rounded under rows of identical helmets.

And after them, a new pattern came, the pattern made as rows of medical orderlies marched out with stretchers.

Kitty and Sarah struggled to balance on the stool they had pushed up against the chink in the shutters at the forbidden windows. Like princesses shut up in their tower in a fairy tale, they were told over and over not to look out of the windows on pain of death. And still they looked out at the densely packed ranks of soldiers and stretcher-bearers marching out.

'How many gaps will there be in those lines tonight?' Kitty whispered, grabbing hold of Sarah's sleeve to keep herself from falling off the chair. It was half-past four in the morning. They knew they wouldn't be called on duty until five, but they knew they wouldn't sleep.

Sarah bolted the shutter at the top and bottom. Then she got down from the stool and sat down again on the edge of her bed. There was no difference any longer between sleeping and waking. There was no such thing as a good night's sleep. They were like birds, sleeping with one eye open, perching on the edge of a very thin branch. In spite of the noise of constant firing and shelling all around them, they fell asleep easily enough now. And then, in spite of the closed shutters deep in an inner room within the castle courtyard, they had both been wakened by the troops creeping around and lining up before they marched out to fight at five.

They dressed in the dark and made their way to the nurses' kitchen. The dim lamplight stung Sarah's eyes at first and she sat in a dream, her hands wrapped around the cup of tea she almost forgot to drink. Kitty's apron was crumpled and grubby and her starched cap had a smear of purple iodine across one corner.

'Do I look a fright like you?' Sarah took a sip of her tea, without milk or sugar. The bitter warmth shot to her stomach and scorched her awake.

'I haven't seen a mirror for three days,' Kitty smiled, 'but you don't look your best and no doubt about it.'

Sarah's thick, dark hair always got more curly when it was steamy and damp, as it was in the kitchens where they had spent their time, sterilizing instruments and washing bandages and making tea. Sarah stood up and the young nurses reached up and made her sit down.

'You've got to eat.'

There was a boiled egg. With salt and half a slice of brown bread with butter. Sarah smiled and sat back in her chair, at home there with the nurses. She felt happier than she ever did in their huge dining room, with her mother fussing round the maid and her father hiding behind his newspaper. More contented than she had ever felt at school in England, where she had more friends around her than at her parents' house. She was happier there, at five o'clock, in the basement kitchen in Dublin

Castle, than she had ever been. She was needed there. She felt at home.

Soon the morning peace was over and they were at full stretch once again.

'Which of you is the nurse? Which one is the helper?'

A sister rushed in, white-faced, the white cuffs on her sleeves already brushed with blood. 'Matron said I'd find one of each in here. And I'll be needing both of you. We've had to set up a new receiving station in the front hall. The fighting's very bad. The worst it's been. They're bringing them in faster than ever now. I don't know how we'll manage. Or how the two of you will face up to it all.' She looked closely at Sarah. 'How old are you, my dear?'

Sarah stood up tall. 'Only a month or two younger than Kitty. I'm the helper. I'll do whatever you need.'

'Have you a cup of tea still in the pot?' The sister sat down suddenly and Kitty poured her tea. 'I haven't slept all night.' She took one sip and smiled, 'I'll be all right again soon.'

Sarah washed the other tea things and the sister sat and sipped her tea as if they had all the time in the world.

'Now,' she sat forward and leaned across the table, 'there's Sinn Feiners coming in now. Stands to reason, the rebels have as many wounded as we have ourselves and there's nowhere else for them to go. But you're not to worry about them. There'll be guards around and they're too ill anyway to do you any harm. Is that all right now? You won't be afraid of them now, will you?'

Sarah grimaced. 'I won't like them,' she said. 'I'll look after them, but I won't like them. You can't like them after all they've done. They say the whole of Dublin's set on fire.'

Her job in the corridors and kitchens near the hall

was to keep the nurses and doctors supplied with boiling kettles to sterilize their instruments. And then there was the endless cleaning. She and Kitty had to keep the areas as clean as they could when all around them soldiers were being brought in, white-faced and bleeding and covered in dust and dirt from burning or shelled-out buildings. The men carrying the stretchers covered the floor with patterns of red-brown footprints from shoes soaked in blood.

Sarah rushed backwards and forwards past the rows of injured men on stretchers and men who were left to lie on the stone floor because the stretchers were needed again. She remembered her mother telling her, months before she first went to the castle as a volunteer, that she wouldn't have to look at an injured man, that a lady shouldn't have to look at anything nasty. On the Sundays when she had helped before, her job had always been to make the tea and nothing else. But now there were injured and dying men and women all around her. She didn't even notice what side they were on. There was nothing she could do except to help them and hope that somewhere out in France another nurse was there to help her brother if he was hurt.

In the dressings room next to the hall, Sarah and Kitty held the bandages and water for the doctors and older nurses. The first soldier Sarah helped to bandage up wasn't badly hurt. The blast from a distant shell had thrown him back up against a wall, but he'd got off lightly with a broken arm while his helmet had stayed on his head and protected him.

'I only landed up here yesterday, nurse. I've never been to Ireland before,' he said. 'Nobody told us where we were going to. All the lads thought we had landed up in France when we got off the ship. But it's not the Germans we've been fighting is it, miss?'

Sarah shook her head and the soldier stood up and moved on as Kitty whispered, 'Look. Over there's a Sinn Feiner.'

But Sarah couldn't make out the man Kitty was trying to point out to her in the constant stream of stretchers coming and going. Another hour went by and then, when it was quiet again for a few minutes and they were allowed to stop and sit down, Sarah asked Kitty to point him out.

'Where's the Sinn Feiner?'

Kitty shook her head. 'Gone. Died before they could do anything.'

She stood up and Sarah followed her through to the corridor which led from the hall. They walked along the row of stretchers covered in blankets until Kitty pulled at a soft hat that was perched on one of the blankets. She lifted back the blanket, just to show Sarah the face. 'That's him.'

The dead man had grey hair. He was older than Sarah's father, too old to join up and fight in France, they would have said. Sarah looked at him for a long time. She wasn't sure what she had expected one of the rebels to look like, but she hadn't expected someone so ordinary, just an old man, like one of her uncles. Then she said, 'Is someone writing down the names of all the dead and wounded? For their relatives. There'll be relatives out looking for all of these people, won't there? Like that American woman who came here on Monday, looking for her daughter.'

They covered the man's face up again, gently, as if he could still take notice of the care they took of him.

They stood back and looked along the line of bodies.

'Do you remember what you said this morning?' Kitty whispered. 'When all those men went marching out? You wondered how many would never come back. How many gaps there would be.'

Sarah was angry. 'They should have been shooting at Germans,' she said. 'All of them. They should have been shooting at Germans over in France. Not here. They shouldn't have Irishmen shooting at the Irish.'

In the afternoon, when matron found out they'd spent the whole morning downstairs with the wounded, she despatched them both upstairs to the ward with its convalescing soldiers home from France. The convalescent ward was calm and quiet and they could take their time again, making tea and spreading bread with butter and raspberry jam.

'You know what you said about somebody taking down names?' Kitty said. 'For all the relatives who'll come looking after this is all over?' She pointed to the soldier who had taken charge the day before. 'Lieutenant Henry's been doing it in the hospital so far. It's just that he can't find out everything they need to know.'

'Don't the men have papers?' Sarah shaved the butter thinly into just enough slices, to make sure that every slice of bread had its share.

'Their clothes get shot off. You've seen the way they look when they come in. They lose their knapsacks. Their pockets get ripped off. Lieutenant Henry told me all about it even before this all started.' Kitty lowered her voice. 'The shells blow them into tiny pieces.'

'But their friends can say who they are.'

'What if their friends have been blown to pieces as well? What if their friends have gone out of their minds like your man over there?'

The tall young soldier they had helped the day before was on the floor again, clinging to the legs of a chair, refusing to get back into bed. He rocked backwards and forwards, clinging to the chair like a lifebelt. 'We're all going back to hell again,' he moaned. 'They'll be sending us all back to France. Why did they let the enemy get

77

so close? Why didn't they stop them? They said we were safe here. They said we were safe.'

Sarah crouched down beside him, Lieutenant Henry on the other side.

'You are safe here,' she said. 'No one will send you anywhere except home when you're better. What's your name?'

She had looked every day for the name card at the end of his bed, but there wasn't one.

Lieutenant Henry tapped at the end of the bed where the name card should have been. 'Er . . . That's something we don't really know,' he said. 'He didn't have anything on him when they pulled him out. It was a total wipe-out. There were bodies on top of him for hours. His best friend was with him, we think. All we know is his accent's from the countryside round Dublin. That's one of the reasons he was shipped back to Ireland when he was well enough to travel. And he seems to respond more when you use the name Michael. So people have been calling him Michael. But you can't be sure when they've lost their mind like this one. Michael could be the name of one of the friends he's lost. Who knows what's going on in his head?'

By six o'clock that night Sarah had had enough. It wasn't the sort of tiredness that would help her sleep. It was simply that she wanted to get away from all the people. So she volunteered to sit in the supper kitchen again, two cushions on the chair to raise her high over the deep sink, and wash bandages, with her back to everyone, ignoring anything they said.

It was quiet now outside, almost as quiet as the garden at home. Then a new sound started up, a gentle, familiar sound, the sound of spades slicing through turf, the sound of earth flying through the air and landing in huge piles, the sound of the castle gardens being dug up.

Sarah climbed up on a chair again, to look out of the high window. It was not quite dark. Where in the morning she had seen row on row of men lining up to march out on the city there were now no more than twenty men with spades, slicing through the turf, making the earth fly through the air behind them onto huge mounds. Beyond that, in the dusk, Sarah could just make out the rows of bodies sewn into sheets and laid out on the paths. The men were digging graves.

She felt very old and very tired. Instead of crying she got down from the window and started her washing again, her back to the door. She took down the stiffest scrubbing brush and attacked the bloodstained dressings she had left soaking in the sink. That was all she could do, get on with life, make sure they looked after the living.

7

Michael swung his arms to keep himself awake, stamped his feet and paced backwards and forwards to stop his eyes from closing. The smoke danced and twirled, whirled around in front of his face in the early evening light of Thursday so you could hardly tell where one building began and the next one ended. Huge buildings that had been standing the night before had been drowned by fire. Nothing was the same any more. The world was cast adrift, forced on by rough waves of fire. Smoke was ebbing and flowing, buildings were appearing and disappearing in each short moment when Michael's eyes fell closed because he was so tired, so very tired.

He was tired, because he'd had to keep awake the whole of Wednesday night, staring into the darkness. He'd scolded himself awake, staring into the mist and swirling smoke early on Thursday morning, after the sun had come up and struggled to throw some light on the damage of the night before. Michael had been on fire watch for two nights now. Buildings all around them had been shelled and caught fire and the fires had raged with no one to fight them. Bands of Volunteers forced to escape from shattered buildings within firing range of the GPO had retreated to the safety of the massive building. With them came more of their wounded, left out on stretchers or on the floor in the basement because it was too dangerous to try and get them to a hospital.

Michael had no idea what was happening anywhere

else in the city. Daisy had been with the women sent out to take messages earlier on in the week, but it was far too risky now for anyone to run the barricades. No news was reaching them. Michael had been there on the first day of the rising when scouts arrived who had covered almost the whole city without going outside, ducking through secret tunnels in cellars, weaving through the gardens of people they could trust. But he knew the Volunteers couldn't get through any more. The houses were gone. Their people were dead. Their network of underground passages between houses was shrinking to a ring of fire.

On Thursday afternoon an officer came round. A tall, thin man he was, with tiny metal glasses perched on his nose and his left arm in a sling.

'Which part of Dublin are you from?' He moved around, asking the same question of all the men and boys on watch. 'Are you from around here?'

But none of them on the watch knew Dublin.

Michael stepped forward and saluted. 'I come from up the country, sir, but I can go out scouting if you'd like me to.'

The officer peered at him and frowned and then said, 'No, no. It's not a scout we need. We have to try and get a priest in tonight.' He turned away and looked round the hall again. There was no one else to ask. He turned back and looked towards Michael again, but he didn't seem to know what to do.

'We've that many wounded and dying. Someone will have to get a priest.'

He gazed out over Michael's head, towards the tall front windows and then shook his head and moved on. John O'Dowd, the oldest soldier still left with them on the watch walked after him, shouting, 'If it isn't safe to go out and get a priest, sir, it won't be safe to take him back the way he came.' But the officer didn't hear him calling out and John turned and walked back to Michael. He pulled his cap off and used the rough outside to wipe away the sweat from his forehead. 'Any priest that's mad enough to come here will have to stay with us till the end. And I mean the end.' Michael couldn't see his face in the shadows, but he heard the crying in his voice. An old man like that, a grown man like that crying. Michael stared at him, trying to make out what he was thinking. He didn't know what to say. What could you say to a grown man crying?

Mr O'Dowd put his cap back on and turned his back on Michael and walked away quietly, very quietly, setting his feet carefully as if he were walking a tightrope. All the Volunteers were quiet now, their shadows flickering on the walls. Michael sat down with his back against a stout table leg and put his hands over his ears without thinking, blocking out the noise that would not go away. The cracking, hissing smoke and the heat and the sharp snapping of the fires made an awful symphony with the screeching of the wounded downstairs in the basement of the great building. The shells beat out a funeral march. All the men on watch waited, with scarcely a word to say. Michael looked all around him, bewildered, as if he were keeping watch over the end of the world.

John O'Dowd walked back on his way across the great hall. 'Are you all right there, Michael?' Michael smiled and stood up again and tried once more to shake himself fully awake.

The smoke and the fires had turned everything to night long before the sun went down, had taken the colour out of the world. In the early evening light the whole of the city was grey and covered with ash. Michael shook his arms and pulled his shoulders back to stop

82

them twitching and jerking with tiredness. Ribbons of smoke wound themselves round him like invisible dancers, forming fantastic patterns in the air, grabbing at his throat and making him cough and rub at his eyes. Immediately in front of him, the shattered, smoke-gilded fragments of glass still left in the huge windows of the GPO gleamed like black diamonds. Michael forced himself to keep moving, keep pacing up and down, keep awake, dodging from one window to the next, catching glimpses of the smoke and the mist outside.

In a daze Michael watched smoke drifting. Sparks leapt up into the sky and then faded away. Smoke twirled and danced across the streets. Black holes gaped at him, sightless eye-sockets where only yesterday he had been looking out at imposing buildings.

Smoke stabbed at his eyes. Smoke swept the sky and swooped like a bird of prey. Smoke crawled like a silent, stalking enemy along the ground, ready to lunge at him and grab him by the throat. There was smoke creeping, smouldering out of the sacks they had piled high as barricades at the GPO windows.

The sacks were on fire.

The sacks were on fire even though he'd watched for two nights so far and nobody had fired directly at them. No shells had landed anywhere near them during his watch. No fires had crept along the barricades across O'Connell Street, no bullets had landed in the mail sacks. Michael had watched and watched and stayed awake the whole time he was supposed to be on watch. Whatever had happened, he hadn't left his post. He hadn't fallen asleep. He was sure he had stayed awake. But in spite of all that the mail sacks were smouldering, smoking, threatening to burst into flame at any moment.

He pressed at his stinging eyes, eyes stinging through smoke and tears, and yelled to wake the sleeping men and to call out to Mr O'Dowd from the other end of the great hall.

'Fire at the front here. Fire at the front.'

As soon as he called out men were there, a great crowd of men with buckets and hoses, drenching the smouldering sacks with water.

'There were no shells, sir. There was no firing.' Michael ran to the officer in charge. 'I didn't miss anything, sir. I don't know where the fire came from. All of a sudden it came. And the sacks were suddenly on fire.'

The officer moved him quickly out of the way.

'You did your best. There was nothing you could do. The heat from the buildings over there made them catch.' And he pointed way over to the other side of O'Connell Street where fires were raging in almost every building that was still left standing.

The men worked without stopping, fighting for their lives, fighting to keep the building they had held for four days. Michael was part of the chain that brought up buckets of water, handing them forward along the line only to see the precious water hissing and turning to steam as soon as it was thrown up against the intense heat at the front of the post office. They fought for hours to stop the fires from taking hold. Michael's face was painted black with a thick paste of soot and steam.

In the early hours of Friday morning, they finally got control. The heat went out of the sacks and only small fires flickered around the front of the building. Michael's long watch was over.

More of the injured had been pulled back into the basement for safety. Michael went down there to find himself a drink and found Daisy, on duty serving out tea and yet more porridge. She was just about to joke with him about the way he looked and then thought better of it, holding out a cup of tea and pointing to her coat, spread out on the floor near one of the pillars. Michael slumped down and reached up for his tea.

'General Connolly came round. On his stretcher. They're not giving up. They're only making plans to move us back.' Daisy carried on serving while she talked.

Michael closed his stinging eyes, sipped his bitter, black tea and leaned back against the pillar. It was good to be there in the half darkness, with people trying to keep their voices down to help to calm the wounded. He was proud of the battle they had fought and won against the flames outside. One of his hands was stinging from the steam burns, but he'd got off lightly. Other men had ended up with their clothes on fire.

'Are you listening, Michael? Or are you asleep?'

He opened his eyes and Daisy carried on talking. 'They want most of the women and girls to get out tonight. But I've said I'm staying. They can't make me go while they still need help with the wounded.'

Still Michael didn't say anything. It hurt his throat to talk and it hurt to think of Daisy getting herself killed along with all the rest of them. He thought she should go. He couldn't get used to the idea that it was all right for a girl to go to war. He raised his head and looked at the state of her. She was wearing a medical orderly's apron over her long white dress, but there was blood on her sleeves and the hem of her dress. Her long blonde hair hadn't seen a comb for four days and the unravelled plaits had collapsed into a cascade of knotted curls, pulled back roughly and tied up with a red-cross armband.

He thought she should go because he didn't want her shot and wounded. Women and girls shouldn't be getting themselves shot. That was an awful thing to see. Wasn't that worse than getting shot yourself—having to see a woman get herself blown to pieces like the ones they'd taken care of in the GPO? He shook himself awake and opened his eyes again.

'You're not listening, are you, Michael? You're half asleep and no surprise about that. But you've got to listen for a minute.'

The queue for tea had gone away and Daisy had time to sit down on the floor next to him. 'Listen, Michael. When General Connolly came round I could tell things had got worse. He didn't say so, but I know they think we'll have to surrender. He said things like, ''Whatever people say about us after this is all over, we've held out against the might of the whole British army for four days''. Now, all that grand talk sounds like he's facing up to surrender. And who knows what will happen then? Get up a minute. It's important.'

She tugged at a corner of her coat. 'Just move yourself along a bit.'

She pulled out her diary, the small book with the black cover and the red leather binding. 'I'm going to write in it tonight and then I'm going to give it to you to look after.'

She pushed at his arm so he nearly fell over. 'You're not to read it, mind.' She opened the book at the first page. 'It goes back to the day my parents brought me to Dublin and then went off up the country to do their work. I said I would keep writing in it, so I could tell them everything I'd been doing.'

'You've only written on one side of each page.'

'That's because I was going to draw pictures as well, things that impressed me on the way.' She laughed. 'But I haven't had much time for drawing yet. And I'm no good at it either.'

She burst out laughing at one of the pages she was reading. 'That was Easter Sunday. Shall I read it to you? No. It was terrible. There I was stuck in that convent. Not a soul in the place except for the nuns and me and those poor Polish girls. But just imagine, if I get killed and if you get killed, one day my poor Polish room-mates could end up reading how mad I was at them.' She ripped the page out cleanly, folding and tearing it into tiny pieces. 'And they're probably not that bad at all. It's not their fault that the nuns think they're saints. And me a dreadful sinner.'

She rolled her eyes in mock horror and then flicked through the rest of the pages. 'I'm going to give this to you to look after. And if you've written a letter to your mother you can give it to me.'

Michael frowned, but she carried on. 'It might be all right. We might both get out of this alive. If both of us get killed, we can't do anything about that. Except,' and she showed him her parents' Boston address neatly written inside the cover of the diary underneath the address of her school in Eccles Street, 'someone might still make sure this gets to my parents.'

Michael didn't say anything. If they were going to die, what chance did bits of paper have, letters and diaries? What chance did paper have when fires were raging all around them? Who would have the time to bother about letters and diaries after it was all over, when hundreds of the dying and wounded were crying out to be looked after?

Michael didn't want to think of surrender. He didn't want to think the way Daisy was thinking. They had both seen people killed that week, both watched wounded Volunteers being carried away on stretchers and never seen again. There were rumours that if they did surrender all the Volunteers would be taken away and shot. But still Michael didn't want to believe that they would die. He talked about it, yes. It was part of being a Volunteer to say you were prepared to die for Ireland. But he didn't see why Daisy should have to die. She hadn't even thought about volunteering until the day she walked into the post office to send a telegram.

He didn't get much sleep again that night. There was no point in trying to sleep with the noise of all that shooting biting into his brain. He dragged himself off to help with a working party that was set to try and tunnel under Henry Street, to make an escape route if they needed to evacuate quickly. But there was no way out. Their escape was blocked. By dawn they had only tunnelled two feet. Michael slumped against a wall and listened as the officers told everyone what he knew already, what they could all see with their own eyes. Any escape from the badly damaged building would have to be out in the open, through the streets to friendly houses, under heavy fire from the British.

The firing on the GPO kept going all night and all morning. There was no sign of Daisy or any of the others left behind. Michael was relieved. They must have managed to get the women and girls to safety. Soon he forgot her. He forgot everything except the bright explosions of light from the snipers still firing at them from every direction and the fires threatening to take hold of the massive building. Then, without any warning, Daisy was suddenly standing beside him, where he was helping to load rifles with the last of their ammunition.

'I need to give you this—like I said.' And she held out her diary. 'I need a letter from you, to take to your parents if I get out of here and you don't.' Her face was filthy and she made it worse as she stood there in front of him, rubbing her fists over her eyes to stop the tears scratched out by the acid smoke that was all around them.

Michael tugged at the lid on a wooden box.

'Not yet.' The lid sprang off and bullets rolled across the

table and onto the floor. 'Not yet. Later. There's too much to do here. Haven't you got enough to do downstairs?'

Daisy slammed her diary down on the table, and ripped out a page for Michael. Then she bent down to pick up a handful of bullets.

'There is no later. You've got to write that letter now. Look at the building. Look at you. There'll be no time once they give us the order to move.'

Michael knelt down to pick up more of the bullets but Daisy was already down on her knees under the table. 'I'll do the bullets. You write the letter.' She rubbed at her stinging eyes with the hem of her dress and then put her head down, hiding her tears, furiously searching for the stray bullets. 'Your mother and father will want to know. My parents will want to know. We have to tell them what it's been like in here. We have to leave something to tell them what we've been fighting for. Now write it.'

'You talk as if we were all going to die.' Michael picked up her pencil. 'We're not going to die. We're going to get out of here. You should have got out of here last night, or this morning, when they told you to.'

Daisy ignored him and slowly crawled around under the table, picking up all the stray bullets. By the time Michael finished the letter to his mother and father, she was smiling again.

> *'Dear mother and father,*
>   *We are here in the GPO in great danger. We*
> *expect the British army to shell us at any moment*
> *today and try to drive us out of the building. If I am*
> *killed, don't worry but pray for me. They brought*
> *in a priest last night, to hear confessions. I am*
> *willing to fight to the last. Pray for me. I have done*
> *something great for Ireland. Goodbye. Your ever*
> *loving son, Michael.'*

Daisy didn't read the letter, but she smiled as she took it from him. She watched until Michael had carefully placed her diary at the bottom of his knapsack.

'Remember. You're not to read it. Just make sure it gets to my mother and father if I get killed.' She had a revolver in her other coat pocket. 'Keep this for me as well.'

She tucked the gun under her diary in his knapsack and then watched as he adjusted the straps from his knapsack and fixed it back on. 'I'm not supposed to carry a gun, looking after the wounded and wearing a red-cross armband. But you might need it. Good luck.'

She turned and walked back to the stone steps into the basement, through the crowd of Volunteers still fighting the threat of fires and helping to load weapons. Her cascade of knotted, silver-blonde hair shone out against her dark coat and then faded away into the darkness, just like all the bright fireworks they had seen that week that flew up into the air and then disappeared.

Daisy was right. There was no time. Michael stood up to follow her as she walked away with his letter. Then a low, whistling noise made him fling himself to the floor again, under the table. A man's voice yelled, 'Get down! Get down!' And there was a noise like claps of wild thunder. Michael curled up, covering his face and his ears, as wood and stone and glass crashed and cracked and shattered and then sprinkled down to the ground in a fine rain of dust that seemed to last forever. There was silence then, a silence Michael had not known since the break of day on that first Monday. A silence full of watching and waiting. The shooting outside had stopped. The falling glass and masonry had settled on the ground. Michael let out a long, slow breath, blew out all the fear he had been hanging on to as he cowered under the heavy wooden table. He took his hands away from his ears and brushed away the dust that had settled on his face, scraping his jaw with a small splinter of glass. He breathed out again, a long sigh that he could hear in the dead quiet. He was alive. He had a scratch on his face.

Then the air began to clear and the silence was broken as Volunteers emerged from the corridors and side rooms. Michael heard the screams of the wounded for the first time. He crawled out from under the table, and stood up rubbing his eyes. Men were shouting and rushing to dig out the Volunteers who'd been hit. A gaping hole in one of the side walls next to a window showed where the shell had hit the building. The officer, with his arm in a sling, moved quickly through the large hall, directing the stretcher-bearers. Only one soldier had been killed. John O'Dowd had been thrown against a wall by the blast.

'He wouldn't have felt a thing.'

Michael's eyes were stinging as he stood and watched one of the stretcher-bearers closing the old man's eyes. There wasn't a mark on him. He and Michael had been doing the same watch the whole time, backwards and forwards, up and down the whole length of the great hall of the GPO. Michael could have walked the great hall of the GPO blindfold, he had paced up and down so often. He could have been killed instead of Mr O'Dowd. He could have been at the end wall where the shell came in instead of down on his knees collecting bullets. He froze and stood and looked at the gaping hole while all around him men and boys were rushing around, shouting, moving the wounded and the rubble, calling for water to put out the fires.

The shell had started a small fire. Someone came up behind Michael and slapped him on his back. 'All right, youngster? Don't stand gaping. Get moving.'

Michael ran away first, right away from the fires and the hole in the side wall to the lobby at the opposite side of the hall. He wanted to open the door, to get right outside and into the open, to breathe fresh air. But that was far too dangerous. He wanted to fling himself down on the floor before he fainted, but it was too late for that. He fell down and was violently sick, his stomach heaving, his insides screaming in pain long after there was nothing more to come.

He sat there, ashamed of himself, but no one noticed. No one had time to notice a boy being sick. Slowly he pushed himself up off the ground and went back to join the crowd of Volunteers fighting to stop the damage spreading, slipping into the chain of men with buckets of water to put out the flames.

They held out until three o'clock in the afternoon, when another shell exploded over the portico. This time the fire grabbed hold of the building and refused to release them from its jaws, raging through a lift-shaft and spreading down into the cellars. One group had to start the evacuation, getting the wounded out and clearing the ammunition they had stored below.

Michael was kept behind with the teams that were fighting fires, while burning shells rained on the building and new fires broke out wherever they turned. They ran with buckets and hoses and the few remaining fire extinguishers. Whenever they brought one fire under control, another one was started immediately by the shelling. While Michael's team continued to struggle against the fires, other soldiers stayed at their post returning enemy fire. Beams were crashing to earth around them, the fires were circling and still they returned the shooting, the zipping of bullets a short, sharp sound in the great symphony of fire.

Michael looked up. The domed glass roof at the rear of the main hall was bending and buckling under the heat. Where the floors of upstairs corridors had already burned away, heavy metal radiators balanced on metal pipes above glowing steel girders, the only parts of the structure not consumed by the flames. He held steady with the hose they were holding and playing on the flames, his whole face and eyes swollen with the heat. They kept on fighting, but the battle was over. The whole of the front of the building had become a furnace. Beams were crashing from the upstairs floors. The glass roof was about to explode and shower them with swords of white heat.

'Move back. Move back.'

The orders echoed around the great hall and still Michael and his small group held fast, passing buckets of water up to the front of the line.

One of the officers came up and grabbed Michael by the shoulder. 'We've an order to move back. Now leave all this and move.'

It was eight o'clock at night and the sky was bright with flames.

They rushed back away from the great hall, to the side entrance into Henry Street where Volunteers on stretchers needed to be moved out. Nobody spoke. Michael looked at the Volunteers left behind, their filthy, smoke-blackened faces shining with the heat. They didn't deserve to die after all they had done. They had held out against the whole might of the British army for nearly a week. He felt sure they were not going to die. And they were not running away. He was not running away. He wanted to live, to escape from the doomed building and find a place of safety where he could live and hide and get ready to fight again.

Michael found himself carrying a stretcher in the last group to leave. He lifted his end of the stretcher and focused on getting across the street to Henry Place. Flames lit their way and trapped them in cages of light so enemy snipers could take aim. Bullets snapped at them like hungry wolves and Michael automatically dodged his body backwards and forwards, protecting the man on the stretcher from the firing.

They turned into Moore Lane and rushed through to pass a barricade over the road while the firing of the British soldiers leaped out at them, growling and biting and snapping at their heels. In the split seconds between bullets, Michael found his head filled with useless outrage. They were firing at people on stretchers. They shouldn't be doing something like that. Wasn't there a law somewhere, some international agreement that said you didn't fire on people who were already wounded? Two of their stretcher cases were prisoners, British soldiers they'd been looking after. Did the British soldiers shooting wildly into the night know what they were doing? Did they know they were firing on wounded British soldiers?

He didn't waste his breath asking anyone. There was no one to ask. Nobody spoke except to gasp out a few words, stepping-stones through the torrent of fire. 'Over to the left.' 'Mind that door.' 'Watch your back.'

It was madness. Why were they shooting on wounded men? Michael and his partner dodged and hopped, ducking into shop doorways, peering out, moving a few steps further. Why was it ending like this? They reached the corner of Moore Lane and Moore Street and Michael staggered and fell. At first he thought he had tripped and hit his foot against the kerb, dropping his heavy load at last because he had carried the stretcher such a long way under fire and they had never stopped to put it down and rest. His brain told his legs to move, told him to stand up and run on again. The bullets snapped and barked around him. He grabbed at his neck with his right hand. A dull ache had started there, as if he had pulled a muscle from carrying the stretcher for such a long time.

He was on his hands and knees. People round him dragged the stretcher handle out of his left hand. Everything was muffled, as if someone had suddenly pulled a thick quilt over his head. There was noise all around, but noise that was getting softer. On his hands and knees still, Michael realized his right hand was wet and held it up so he could look at it, but he couldn't see his own hand. He moved it closer to his face, but he couldn't see it. All he could see was a bright, white light, thin and shining like a bullet coming straight towards him, seeking him out in the darkness.

Then everything went dark.

8

Doctor Donnelly told Sarah to stick her tongue out.

'Have you slept at all this week?' He shook his head and waved his finger at her. 'Your mother will never forgive me if you get yourself all worn out.'

Sarah pulled a face. 'You're saying I look old and ugly, aren't you?'

'No. Just that you look like a girl who hasn't slept all week.'

Sarah wiped the corner of her apron across her whole face, so he shouldn't see even the beginnings of the tears she had been holding back. She wasn't going to give up now. Doctor Donnelly had brought good news of her family. None of them had been caught up in any of the dangerous parts of the city. They were all safe. Her brother James was safe in England, back from France for a week. His unit would not be allowed back home to Dublin because of the troubles.

'Do they know where I am?' Sarah had scarcely had time to think about her family.

'Your father knew Mr Delaney got you here safely. And he just kept saying you're a sensible girl, very well able to look after yourself.'

Sarah scrubbed her face with her apron again.

'Look at the state of me. You wouldn't believe this apron was white when I got here on Monday.'

'I must say, if you'd been my daughter I would have been a bit more worried about you.' The doctor sat down heavily on one of the small stools in the kitchen. 'It's been a hard week for anyone, let alone a young woman of your age. How old are you now?'

'Nearly fourteen.'

'It'll probably be safe for you to go home in a few days, now they've surrendered.' Bullets whizzed past the supper room window in quick succession. More bullets, it seemed, than they had heard before the ceasefire. The doctor made as if to duck. 'But not straight away. The streets aren't safe for anyone yet—let alone a girl as young as yourself.'

'I don't want to go home,' Sarah said. 'I'm afraid my mother and father will never let me come back here, once they see the state I'm in. I shan't be telling them anything I've seen or done. I want to come back, and I want to be a doctor like you one day. There! I've said it.'

The door opened and closed quietly as an older nurse perched herself on the stool at the end of the table, grabbed a teacup and poured herself a tiny amount of tea, just enough to take a quick sip. Then she stood up again.

'More new arrivals, doctor. They need you again downstairs. Some of the rebels.' The nurse winced. 'They say the authorities want us to patch them up so they can shoot them. I've heard they're shooting anyone over the age of fifteen. The poor young idiots who got themselves caught up in all this fighting for Ireland. Their poor mothers.'

Sarah rushed downstairs after the two of them. In the receiving room the swing doors were constantly battered, backwards and forwards, backwards and forwards, by the torrent of new arrivals.

Matron stroked her hand over the unconscious white face of a very young boy; one of the rebels, they said. The whole of his upper body from the neck down, the whole of the stretcher, was covered in blood. She rested her hand on his forehead and looked at him for a long time, as if there were no one else to see to, as if looking at him would somehow bring him back out of the darkness.

'At least he's so young that they won't want to shoot him.'

Doctor Donnelly took over. 'It looks as if they won't be needing to.'

He felt for a pulse in the boy's arm. Then he pulled out a knapsack that someone had wedged underneath the young soldier on the stretcher, in the small of his back.

'He can't be very comfortable with this here,' he said, 'if he can feel anything at all.' He handed the knapsack to Sarah. 'Here, Sarah, my dear. Can you take this and get it cleaned up and see if you can find out his name.' He shook his head. 'We're going to need to find his relatives.'

Sarah looked quickly at the boy on the stretcher. The same age as her, he must be, if that. Younger than she was perhaps, with a thin, white face that made him look as if he hadn't eaten for several weeks. She had lost count now of the number of soldiers she had seen arriving, like this one, barely alive. She looked again at his poor young face. One of the Sinn Feiners. One of the violent, evil men who had caused all the death and destruction of the last week. An enemy of the people. She couldn't hate him. She watched as he disappeared, surrounded by the two nurses, the doctor and his assistant, rushing him into the room they had had to use as an operating theatre.

She was still clutching the filthy knapsack. There was no place to clean it in the receiving room, with new cases arriving every few minutes. By the look of it she would have to try to rescue what she could from the bag and then throw it away. She clutched it tightly, glad that she had forgotten to take off the blue and white kitchen apron she had been wearing. That at least had protected the rest of her clothes from the stripes of blood and soot that covered her kitchen apron where she had been clutching the bag to her chest. She frowned and looked at her right hand, covered in the blood still seeping out of the bag. She had been holding it far too closely as if that way she could stop the young soldier from slipping away from them and dying.

Sarah was alone in the supper room kitchen when she finally put the bag down. She washed her hands carefully, slowly, and staying very calm, like all the grown-ups she had seen that week. Keeping calm, staying in control. But however hard she tried to stop them, the tears would come. 'You great baby.' She looked down at her apron, trying to find a clean corner to wipe her eyes. 'You're not the one who's got hurt.' She had to take a great sniff and realized she was talking aloud to herself.

'Look at you. There's not a mark on you. Look at you crying like a baby and all those men down there with their legs blown to pieces. Stop crying. Stop crying.'

She thumped the draining board with her fists and the more she shouted at herself the harder it was to stop. So she gave in. She let herself go over in her mind the sights she had seen that week and then the sight of the white-faced young Sinn Feiner, the boy without a name, the whole of his body covered in blood, a young boy who was going to die for certain and was only the same age as her.

'Why am I crying for someone I don't even know?' She put her face in her hands and sobbed so loudly that people would have come running if there had been anyone left upstairs to hear her. 'Why am I crying for the enemy?'

She couldn't hate him.

When she was all wrung out, when she had cried until her head stung and her nose was blocked and her eyes were red and swollen, she splashed her face over and over again with cold water. She took her cap off and held her head under the cold water tap and let it splash all over her hair and neck. Then she battered her forehead with her cold, wet hands, trying to smooth away the headache. It got better, but it didn't go away. She knew she would have to drag herself around for the rest of the day, so tired she could have lain herself down anywhere and fallen asleep.

But there was work to be done. The filthy canvas knapsack was lying where she had left it, on the draining board. As she moved it towards her, her hands were once again covered in streaks of soot and blood. But it had to be done. She opened the two buckles and lifted up the flap. Everything inside was soaked. The canvas the bag was made out of was so coarse that everything, dust and water, soot and blood and splinters of glass had gone right through. She wondered if she would be able to read a name even if there was one inside. Right at the top of the bag there was a tightly sealed tin box with a red cross in a white circle on the lid.

Inside the box everything was clean, untouched, never used. There was a small jar of ointment. There was a very small pair of scissors. There was a roll of sticking plaster and there were three sparkling clean, tightly rolled up bandages, none of them bigger than the sort you might use to bind up a cut hand. Sarah started to cry again. Who had given that boy a first-aid kit when he set off to be a soldier? Who had ever led him to believe that the clean and tidy little tin box of equipment would help to keep him alive? She stared at the contents of the box without touching them and cried again, raging at the empty room. Then she remembered her headache and how she was trying to clear the fog away from her brain and she forced herself to stop crying.

There was no name inside the first-aid box. She closed it, then took a cloth and gently wiped the outside of the box clean. She set it apart from the bag, on the right hand side of the draining board. There was a metal bottle next in the bag. It was empty, but it must have had milk in it at one time. She washed that out and cleaned it carefully before putting it beside the first-aid box. She started to picture the boy's mother, receiving the last items of his kit when she was told he was dead, and decided that the least she could do was to clean out the knapsack, to take away some of the signs of the battle.

The soldiers sometimes carried rations with them in their packs, but there was no sign of food in this one. Sarah had overheard the soldiers in the yard saying that if the rebels had not been forced into surrender by heavy shelling, they would probably have been starved out of their hiding places. She pulled a notebook out of the bag, its pages glued together with blood. All she could do for the moment was to carefully mop the outsides and the spine of the book and leave it to dry. She would probably find the name of the soldier somewhere inside the little black notebook with its red spine, but she didn't want to risk tearing at the pages while they were still wet, so she left it beside the other things on the draining board.

At the bottom of the knapsack was a small revolver. Sarah pulled it out of the bag. If they knew he was still carrying a gun after the surrender, wouldn't they shoot him? It didn't matter. He was going to die anyway. He had probably died when they tried to operate on him. But his parents would get into more trouble if their son still had a revolver on him when he was found. Sarah pictured the boy's mother being told he was dead. Didn't she have trouble enough?

She jumped up and ran to the door of the supper room kitchen. The corridor outside was deserted. Everyone must be downstairs attending to the new patients. Sarah still had the gun in her hand. She ran back and put it down at the bottom of the bag. No, that wouldn't do. The bag was too heavy. Someone would know who it belonged to, would know there was a weapon inside. She couldn't just leave it in the bag. She took the gun out of the bag again and wiped it clean as best she could. Then she took a clean apron down from the small pile still left on the shelf, folded it over the gun and then over her arm and walked out into the corridor.

'I'm just going to get myself a wash.'

That was what she was going to say if she met anyone on the way to the nurses' room. But there was no one around. She hid the gun inside her own small bag, pushed it under the bed, and crept back along the corridor to the kitchen. She threw the knapsack into a sink of cold water and watched as the blood flowed out of it. Over and over she emptied the water out of the sink and still the blood came seeping out of the bag. In the end, she left it to soak and climbed up onto a stool to arrange the boy's few possessions along the shelf above the window. She managed to separate some of the middle pages of the notebook, but there was nothing written inside them. She wondered if he had started writing in the book at the beginning of the week.

There was a loud noise down in the yard outside. A noise of soldiers being called to stand to attention. Then Sarah heard the sound of running footsteps in the corridor outside. Kitty pushed open the door.

'They're bringing Connolly in. You know, one of the Sinn Fein generals. They've got him down in the yard. He's one of the wounded. Have a look out. You'll see him from there. He doesn't look like a villain. Have a look.'

Sarah opened the window. The sound she had heard, of soldiers being called to stand to attention, was the sound of Connolly's own soldiers, three on each side of his stretcher. There were thirty or forty British soldiers standing all around the yard as well, all with their weapons trained on the unarmed rebels. Sarah stood watching for at least ten minutes, waiting for the crowd around the head of the stretcher to move aside so she could see the rebel general, but nothing happened. Then she decided to go down to the yard and see the man for herself.

She ran down the stairs and along the corridor until she got to the main door into the yard, where they were still receiving new patients. The streets were safer now but that meant there was more work for them as far more of the wounded were finally getting through to the hospitals. Matron was standing near to the door of the yard.

'Haven't they got you home yet?' she said. 'Well, as long as you're here, you can help with the men upstairs. Everyone's forgotten them in all the troubles we've got down here. Off you go, young lady. There's too much for you to see down here and too much for us to do. We've no time for anyone to stand around gawping.'

A stretcher was rushed in, the man on his back with a dressing covering the whole of one side of his face. They said he'd been shot through the head. Sarah stepped back out of the way, but she managed to ask before she was moved back upstairs, 'Why are they all waiting outside? Why is Connolly out there in the yard with all those men when he's wounded?'

One of the soldiers on stretcher duty nodded in the direction of the British army headquarters. 'They're trying to decide whether they shoot him now or patch him up first and then do it later.'

Matron walked over to him and glared. 'Our job is to look after the sick,' she said. 'Let the lawyers look after the law. Now, will you get on with your job, young man, and less of your gossip.'

Sarah walked upstairs again with Kitty.

'They don't know where to put the general, you know.' Kitty knew everything that was going on. 'That's why they're keeping him so long in the yard.' She grinned. 'They're scared he'll hop away on the one good leg he's got. But I've heard both his legs are shot to pieces.'

She shrugged her shoulders and ran ahead of Sarah to the ward kitchen.

'Come on. They'll be dying for a cup of tea.'

The men in the convalescent ward were quiet. There was none of the joking Sarah had got used to in her visits before. Some of the seriously wounded men from the week's fighting had had to be moved to the ward full of men recovering after France and a blanket of shock and despair blacked out their good spirits.

In the night two more had been brought in, a man who had had his arm amputated and a young boy, a British army soldier who the nurses said was dying. They had tried to calm him down but every ten minutes he would sit up straight in his bed and stare at a world he could not see. Sarah wondered what had happened to the young Sinn Feiner they had brought in early that morning, but there was no point in asking. In those mad days after the surrender the wounded, the dead, and the dying rushed through the castle hospital like riderless horses in one mad race for the finishing line.

She and Kitty, alone in the ward, continued to change dressings and give the men their tea or water. They were so short of nurses and doctors that Sarah sometimes had to hold the men down while they were given injections of morphia.

When they could tell that the young British army soldier was dying, Kitty sent for one of the student doctors and an older nurse. But there was nothing they could do. The chaplain arrived, a Church of England chaplain because the young soldier had only arrived from England to join the fighting the day before.

'What if he's Irish?' Sarah stood in the doorway of the ward as the chaplain stepped outside the screens around the bed. 'What if he's Catholic?'

'Ah, sure what does all that matter if he's dying? The Lord's not going to keep him out if he was blessed by the wrong man now, is he?'

Kitty and Sarah left the doctor and the chaplain to their work and went over to where the tall young soldier they called Michael was out of bed again, shivering on the floor, his teeth chattering as he repeated the fear he couldn't let go of. 'They're going to send us back into hell. This is like France again. They're going to send us back to France as soon as we can walk.'

They managed to get him back into bed and Sarah stood over him, stroking his frightened eyes closed while she watched the screens close around the bed of the soldier who was no more than a boy. He had died fighting for the British army even though he was Irish. She remembered her own words, only a few days before, 'If only they were fighting the Germans, not their fellow Irishmen.' She had had enough of it.

Why were they fighting at all?

The man who had had his arm amputated that day screamed out in pain and Kitty and the sister rushed over to his bed. Sarah stayed to reassure 'Michael', the young boy who was so plagued with the nightmare he lived through in the trenches that he couldn't remember his name and couldn't sleep. She thought of the mothers and fathers of all these men. Why had they let them fight?

Her mother and father and all their friends had even been cheering when their parade of young men, their sons, had set off to fight the Germans. Sarah's head started to ache again. She would have to lie to her parents about what she had seen, so that they wouldn't stop her coming back to work in the castle. But perhaps she was wrong. Perhaps she should tell them, tell the whole world. If everyone could see what she had seen that week, in that madhouse of sawn-off limbs and bodies sewn into sheets, of living men driven mad and dying men with no names, how could any of them ever again say it was right to take up arms and fight?

When the night-staff came on duty, Sarah crept back into the supper room kitchen, climbed up onto her stool and looked at the first-aid box, the metal bottle, and the notebook she had left out to dry on the shelf. Three poor things to show for a whole young life. Treasures for the soldier's parents if she could find out who they belonged to. The pages of the notebook were still glued together, apart from two or three unwritten pages in the centre. She left the book open, and then opened the window to let some fresh air into the room. The sun was setting outside, painting the sky blood red. It was less than a week since Easter Monday. Only a week ago she had set off from home to help out at the castle serving tea.

The world had changed. She had changed. They might make her go back home, but her parents' world wasn't her world any more. Nothing now would ever be the same.

9

'**M**y darling, you look frightful. Have you had the most awful time?'

Sarah's mother gave her a peck on her forehead. 'But it's so good to have you back home. Get Mrs Delaney to heat water for a bath and then put some proper clothes on. You can tell us all about it after lunch.'

She had walked in just when her mother was holding a meeting of the Committee for the War Effort. Her mother's friends, all the committee, shook their heads and said how very worrying it must have been to have Sarah in the centre of Dublin that week, but her mother just smiled and told them how sensible Sarah could be. Then she said, 'And she couldn't have been anywhere safer than Dublin Castle, the headquarters of the British command, now could she?'

Sarah had looked at herself properly for the first time in one of the huge, gilded mirrors when they were able to walk through the castle throne room again in broad daylight. She'd not had clean clothes for a week and all the nurses had washed themselves in the kitchens whenever they had time.

'You know, the thing that was worrying me all week was that they might have put her with some of the wounded or that she might have seen something. Not right for a young girl. Not right at all. But the captain told me—the nice young man who brought her home—he told me she'd been on duty serving tea. Well, there's nothing wrong with that, now, is there?'

The captain travelling on to the north had been Sarah's only chance to get home that week, and matron had persuaded her she ought to go, however much she argued against it. Sarah wanted to get back to the hospital and she was afraid her mother would try to keep her at home.

She closed the drawing room door behind her and left them to their meeting. Only a week had gone by but her parents' house felt like a foreign country. With her bedroom window thrown wide open it was quiet enough to hear the birds singing, quiet enough to make out different birds, with different tunes. She wondered what the week had been like for her mother and her parents' friends out there in the countryside at the far edge of the city. The newspapers had not arrived all week, which had annoyed Sarah's father. He must have picked up what was happening because of his work as a doctor but Sarah's mother had heard nothing of the fighting. And what she had not seen or heard had done very little to disturb her peace.

Sarah stood with her bedroom window open and listened to the singing of birds instead of bullets. After a week of sleeping on camp beds with only standing room between them, she stood in her huge bedroom and listened to the gentle sounds of work in the kitchen, Mrs Delaney whisking eggs in her copper bowl, the maid scratching away at the potatoes. She lifted the secret compartment in the one drawer she could lock in her desk and hid the young soldier's gun, wrapping it first in a gold-coloured silk scarf. Then she went downstairs and stood outside the drawing room, listening to the gentle hum of gossip while her mother and her friends knitted and chatted about the war effort. More apprehensive than she had been in any of the corridors when they were under rebel fire, Sarah went in to face the group of knitting women.

'There, she looks better than she did earlier.' Her mother patted the sofa beside her, signalling Sarah to sit down. 'Though she still looks frightful, doesn't she?'

Sarah was always nervous when her mother's friends were there, talking about her and looking at her clothes, her hair, her complexion. They talked about all young girls like that, as if they were part of a collection of dolls kept in a glass cabinet and taken down once or twice a year to be admired.

'You need to be careful with your looks, dear.'

One of her mother's friends had married off two of her daughters already and knew what she was talking about.

'You've had an awful experience this week, Sarah—but you must make sure it doesn't affect your looks. Come over here. Let me look at you.'

She pinched at Sarah's cheeks and patted them.

'You know, what Sarah needs is a trip to France, to one of those spas.' Then she put her hands up to her face in horror. 'But you can't travel nowadays, can you? You can't do anything, with this dreadful war on.'

'I'm just very tired,' Sarah said. 'It was rather too noisy for sleep, wherever we were. And we had to keep moving.' She went over to the door, desperate to make her escape. 'Can I be excused, mother?'

Her mother waved her hand. 'You rest, my darling.' And Sarah heard her laughing as she was closing the door. 'They call it "beauty sleep" now, don't they?'

Sarah didn't go back to her own room. She had come home, but she didn't feel at home. She couldn't stay there, now everything had changed. She went to her mother's dressing room and took down the second Red Cross uniform her mother had bought when she first started to volunteer at the castle. There was another bright white apron and the starched cap that tied with a bow under her chin. There was the long, blue wool dress her mother had never worn. In her mother's drawer were the starched and frilled cuffs she would need to roll up her sleeves and keep them out of the water when she was washing.

She dressed carefully and slipped into her father's study. Her father had been working when she arrived, but she pulled him out from the depths of his study to tell him that she was home, safe and well.

'You said I had a week to show you I can work hard. Well, I've done that. I have worked hard and hardly slept the whole week. Then you said you would talk to mother about me not going back to school.'

Her father put down his pen.

'Well now, look. I know I did say we could talk about you leaving school early, but if you're really serious about leaving school properly, it would have to be more than a week just serving teas.'

He sat back and swivelled round to look properly at his daughter.

Sarah looked straight back at him. She wanted to tell him everything about the week she had just spent at the hospital, about the dead and the dying and the men back from the trenches driven out of their minds. But then they might never let her go back. She just stared at her father. What did he know? He was a country doctor, with rich patients coming to him with coughs and colds. How could he know what it was like?

He nodded. 'It's been more than a week of just serving teas, hasn't it?' Then he whispered, 'We won't tell your mother what it's like in Dublin.'

He turned to his desk and carefully sorted the papers he had been working on. 'I'll come with you.' Sarah was about to protest when he said, 'Not to the castle. I've no doubt the army posts are well provided for. But there'll be

110

other hospitals where they'll be needing doctors. The patients out here can do without me for a week or two.'

While her father went to speak to her mother, Sarah slipped down the back stairs, where Mrs Delaney was busy with the maid, cooking lunch.

'Oh, Miss Sarah, you look a picture in that uniform. Doesn't she look a treasure?'

Sarah smiled. 'I can't stay here, Mrs Delaney. I'm going back to help at the hospital. They need me. You will look after mother, won't you? She'll understand. And can Mr Delaney take us to the outskirts of the city in the car?'

Mrs Delaney packed her a basket of food. Then Mr Delaney drove with Sarah and her father as far as he could until the road blocks started. Once they reached the city hospital, Sarah left her father to help out there. Then at last she was on her own again, walking the last few miles to the castle. The red cross fastened to her sleeve gave her a free passage and nobody asked her where she was going as she moved from one barricade to the next. But nothing had prepared her for the wreckage and desolation.

She wondered at how little she had noticed, as they had driven out of Dublin early that morning. She had been talking non-stop to the captain, about her brother James and about what it was like in France, and they had sped past the ruins and the fires still burning.

Now she was walking through battlefields, through streets where not a single building was left standing. Roads were like stony beaches, rough with the shingle of broken bricks and tiles and the wreckage of burnt-out cars and carts. Shop windows untouched by fire displayed their daggers of shattered glass, all that was left behind by the looters. Houses and department stores loomed out of the smoke like giant skeletons, their burnt-out windows

111

the staring eyes and grinning mouths. Crowds of people stood around, in shock, staring at ruined shops and cars.

Everything had changed. And nobody was trying to change things back to the way they were before. Around Nelson's column, people were standing with handkerchiefs over their mouths to keep out the smell of death. At first, Sarah thought they were just there to stare at the dead horses, some lying flat, some with feet in the air. But they were reading the white posters at the base of the pillar—the proclamations the rebels had pasted all over the city, To The People of Ireland from the Provisional Government of the Irish Republic. Sarah pulled her apron up over her mouth and she too read the proclamation:

'IRISHMEN AND IRISHWOMEN:

In the name of God and of the dead generations from which
she receives her old tradition of nationhood, Ireland,
through us, summons her children to her flag and strikes
for her freedom.'

All around the pillar that soared in memory of Nelson, the great British admiral, the city was in ruins. Sarah stepped back to let other people through to read the proclamation and walked on. She wanted to take one look at the post office, the place she had heard was the centre of all the fighting, before taking the direct way to the castle. But she had to ask a woman to show her the way first, lost in her own city.

'It's just there, in front of you. Will you look what those idiots got up to? We've not had bread nor milk for a week.' The woman had a toddler clinging to her, wrapped in her shawl. 'Look. There's our great post office. Will you look at their grand flags.'

The GPO was black, when Sarah remembered it as a

soaring white stone building with statues over the portico. The tattered, scorched Irish Republican flag still floated proudly above the building but most of the statues were broken. They were pulling down buildings already in O'Connell Street, because of the danger if they were left standing. As Sarah stood and looked at the green, white, and gold flag floating above the post office, a small group marched round the corner. British soldiers had mounted guard over a group of Volunteers and they were being marched away to prison, one of the last groups to surrender. People jeered and spat at them. The woman with her child in a shawl leaned over to Sarah.

'Hanging's too good for them. And shooting's too quick.'

An old woman picked up a handful of stones and threw them all at the line of prisoners. 'I hope they all rot in an English jail.'

Sarah saw boys of her own age among the prisoners, young men like her brother, James, and men as old as Mr Delaney who had been told he was too old to sign up and fight in France. She thought of the young boy they had taken into her hospital the night before. She couldn't bear to look at the men there, bravely marching, some of them even smiling at the jeering crowd.

'They're all going to be shot, as soon as the army get them off to prison.'

Two very thin old men sat on the edge of the pavement outside the remains of a public house, looking up at the line of prisoners marching past.

'And good riddance to them.'

'Ah but, wouldn't you think, if they wanted to get themselves killed, they'd have joined up with a proper army and fought the Germans?'

Everyone was pleased to see Sarah back at the castle. She had come home. The nurses told her she was looking well after her day out and the men who could walk about on crutches told her they had missed her while she was gone. The ceasefire had brought a steady stream of new cases arriving at the hospital and she was sent straight up to join Kitty on the wards.

In the one day she had been away, everything had changed. The bed where the young British soldier had died the night before she left had screens around it once again. Another soldier was dying, would be dead before morning.

'They don't know whether this one is British or one of the Sinn Feiners.'

Kitty grabbed hold of Sarah's basket of food so they could hide it in the supper kitchen. 'He's the same age as you and me. Looks too young to be a soldier. There was too many wounded came in at one go and they lost count of which side they belonged to.' She shook her head. 'He's holding on, but they don't think he'll last.'

When they'd done serving all the men their lunch, Sarah peeped inside the screen. Very clean now, with a huge bandage around his throat and around his terribly thin ribcage, but with a face even paler and whiter than when she first saw him, Sarah recognized the young soldier whose bag she had been told to clear out when they first brought him in. There was no name at the end of his bed, so they obviously hadn't been able to find anything in his uniform to identify him. There were no other Sinn Feiners in the ward, nobody who could have given him a name. If he lived they would put him in prison for years. Some people were still saying all the rebels were going to be shot. Sarah went and got the ward sister.

'I was there when they brought this one in.' They walked over to the bed and slipped inside the screens. 'We couldn't find his name. But he's not one of the

114

rebels. He's a British soldier.' She stroked her hand over his head, but there was no response at all and she watched while the ward sister wrote on the note at the end of his bed.

The young soldier's breathing stopped sometimes, long enough for her to count to ten, and then spluttered back to a slow, natural rhythm again. Sarah stood and looked at him for a long time and then let the curtains close around his bed.

The little notebook, high up on the shelf in the supper room kitchen, was drying out so that she could begin to separate the pages. The last two pages that had been written on dated back to the Wednesday and Thursday of the previous week, the 26th and 27th April 1916. Did that mean the boy had been shot on Thursday night and then left almost to bleed to death until Saturday when they had brought him in to the hospital? The whole thing was madness. The boy was going to die when he might have been saved if they'd managed to get him straight away to a hospital.

Sarah climbed down from the draining board and the chair she needed to reach the high shelf, sat facing the door and started to read the entry for Thursday, 27th April. The young soldier had clearly been inside the GPO, because he wrote of the sniping around O'Connell Street and the first shell that fell nearby around midday. None of the shells hit the building, but they caused so many fires around it that the heat was driving them back. That was the last entry. 'The enemy are surrounding us with artillery fire, but we intend to keep fighting to the end.' And then the young soldier had written, 'This comes with my love to you, my dear mother and father. I will give it to a fellow Volunteer for safe keeping. If you are reading this, it means I have died for Ireland. Be proud of me.'

Sarah put the notebook down on the table. If the soldier in their ward was the Volunteer who had received the book for safe keeping then she was even further away from finding out his identity. She tried to separate the first few pages from each other, to see if she could read the name at the front, but they were still glued together. She would have to do the job very slowly.

Slowly she climbed from the chair on to the draining board and put the notebook in its hiding place at the back of the high shelf. The madness of it all. They would probably never find out the name of the young soldier behind the screens. They would have to bury another young boy with no name. And his poor parents would never know what had become of him.

Sarah went back to the ward. Michael, the tall young soldier from France, was out of bed again. They couldn't keep him still whatever they tried. It was a blessing he didn't do anyone any harm. This time, before Sarah could get to him, he had opened the screens around the young Sinn Feiner. They both stood and looked at the boy in the bed for a long time. Then Sarah put her hand on the young man's shoulder to steer him back to his own bed. He pushed her away and looked at her in horror.

'Has he been in France as well, nurse? He's too young. He shouldn't have gone to France. Why are they making boys that young do their fighting for them?'

10

T he shooting stopped on Wednesday after the surrender. After that the days slipped away quietly, gliding gently into each other where they had tumbled along in a great torrent, a rush of life and death, the week before. Now it was rumours that flew about like snipers' bullets. Rumours that three of the leaders of the provisional Irish government had been taken out and shot at dawn only four days after the surrender.

'They say they're shooting the rebels as soon as they catch them.' Lieutenant Burns, the newest young army doctor from England had only arrived in Ireland in March. He came to their kitchen for cups of tea and brought them all the news.

'Ach! You listen to a load of nonsense. Who told you that now?' Sister Dawson slapped a hunk of cake onto the tea plate she banged down on the table next to him. 'They don't know what they're talking about, whoever they are. There's such a thing as justice now, isn't there? There'll be a trial an' all. Now eat up and get back to your work, all you young things, and less of your gossip.'

The men in the wards upstairs were talking about it too. Some said there hadn't been time for a proper trial, so they couldn't have had executions yet. Some said you didn't need a proper trial when you were at war. Then they argued about whether Britain was at war with the Irish and the English soldiers joked that they didn't want to go to war with the Irish nurses. Nobody really believed that they would shoot the rebels once they had surrendered.

Then a copy of the *Irish Times* arrived in the nurse's kitchen and there was no mistaking the news. The headlines screamed like a sergeant bawling on parade:

SEDITION MUST BE ROOTED OUT OF IRELAND

That's when they found out that eight of the rebel leaders had already been executed, shot at dawn in Kilmainham Jail. Sarah leaned over Kitty's shoulder while she read the reports. Hundreds of Irish men and women had been sent away to prisons in England.

Back on the ward, the British soldiers whispered the news and stopped talking when Sarah drew near. But she heard them all the same. There was no more joking now about Britain and Ireland being at war. The Irish had raised an army to fight the British. The British soldiers, being looked after by Irish nurses in an Irish hospital bed, spoke with respect of the Irish army. Eleven hundred Irish Volunteers with the strange assortment of guns they had been able to get hold of had held out for five days against more than twelve thousand of the British army, with their heavy artillery and their gunboat on the River Liffey. Nobody could understand how they had held out against the might of the British army. But the Irish had held their own capital city for five days and now the British government were making them pay for it.

Sarah went about her work. At the hospital they gave her the changes of uniform she needed now the laundry was back working again, so she didn't have to go home for clean clothes. She was losing track of the days.

'I expect you'll be going back to school soon.' Kitty bent down to check they had everything the nurses needed on the dressings trolley, before they pushed it together along the corridor towards the ward. Sarah frowned. It was the first time she had thought of home for days. She knew she would have to go home some time, as soon as they sent for her, but no one had come. It was almost as if she had already gone back to school in England and her parents were getting on with their normal life. She shrugged her shoulders. 'I've told them I'm not going back.' Kitty stood up, about to protest, when Sarah stopped her.

'You've no place to tell me, Kitty. You left school as soon as you reached twelve. And that's what I want to do.' Kitty opened her mouth to speak and Sarah ran back into sister's room to get the iodine.

She had never felt more at home, never felt more useful, never found anything she wanted to do more than the work she had done in the hospital. She had changed. She didn't want Kitty lecturing her. And she could never go back to the school where the teachers lectured her every day on what a young lady should do or a young lady shouldn't do.

'My mother wants me to stay at her English school so I can learn how to be a young lady.' She put the bottle down on the lowest shelf of the trolley, next to the white enamel bowls. 'They want to find me a suitable young man and marry me off.' She groaned and then stood up straight, grabbing on to her end of the heavily laden trolley. 'But I don't want to marry some boring English man. And I don't want to go to school in England. This is where I belong.'

Kitty put her fingers to her lips just in time as two British soldiers appeared along the corridor behind Sarah, nodding to them as they walked past.

'You've got to be careful how you talk.' Kitty stopped the trolley and leaned across the bandages to whisper. 'They weren't visitors, you know.' Her voice dropped even further. 'They were guards.'

Sarah didn't care. She wasn't afraid of the British. Her mother wanted her to be more like them, to be a young English lady. But young Irish women were different now, different to the English they were supposed to admire. Irish women had carried guns and fought for their country. Sarah had seen them arriving with the emergency convoys before they were moved on to the women's hospital. If they could fight for freedom for their country, Sarah could fight for the freedom not to be locked up in an English school.

There were British guards everywhere and everyone said it was because General Connolly was still in the castle. The doctor who saw him every day was another one of those who came in and had his tea on their ward.

'There's never fewer than ten British soldiers outside his room.' He was a long, thin man from the West of Ireland with an Oxford accent. Sarah leaned across the table, trying to catch his whispering. 'The man can hardly sit up, let alone walk out of his room and escape. And they've got ten soldiers guarding him. That's the might of the great British army for you.'

'That's dangerous talk, young man.' The ward sister bustled in and started off clearing the tea things. 'Now, if you'll be so kind, you'll take yourself off back to your own patients.'

The young Sinn Feiner on Sarah's ward was clinging to life. He had opened his eyes once, so the nurses took turns sitting by his bed and talking to him whenever they had time to stop. Sarah was sitting beside him one day soon after the first executions, when the ward sister came to get her. 'I'm sorry. You're wanted in matron's rooms.'

In all the week of the troubles, Sarah had never been in matron's rooms. She had only ever seen matron moving around in the corridors, calmly explaining what had to be done, telling nurses to sit down when they had been on their feet for eight hours, making sure everyone had enough to eat, watching over her flock like a shepherd. Matron sat waiting for Sarah in a large room with a high ceiling and a sofa that matched the flowered curtains. A woman was sitting on the sofa, dressed in white and with a white parasol. It was the American woman Sarah had first seen on the morning of Easter Monday.

'Sarah, we need you to help in the search for a girl who's gone missing. A girl about your age. You were in the receiving station when the women patients were brought in—before they moved them on to other hospitals?'

Sarah frowned and sat down. 'There were so many people after the surrender . . . I don't remember any of the women very much. There were some young girls, but I don't remember their faces. It all happened so quickly. Doctor looked after some of the worst and then the rest were moved on. They were all moved on as quickly as they could be.'

'We needed the space.' Matron was still searching through a register of names she had tried to keep during that chaotic week. 'All the women and girls were moved on, you see. I'm afraid we don't know which of the hospitals they were taken to next. It was just—'

The woman interrupted her. 'She must be somewhere.'

The American accent matched her expensive clothes. The woman stood up and walked over to the window, as if she was going to see her daughter just outside. 'I came here the first time because I hoped to find her alive. They said I should look in the hospitals and this was the first hospital I came to before it all started. It's the first one I've looked in since the surrender. She must be somewhere.' She looked at Sarah. 'You're so like her, my dear. That's what matron said when I showed her my daughter's picture, and she's right. Can you come with me? I'm sure it will help people remember. I'm sure we'll find her.'

Matron shook her head. 'There are hundreds of people missing.' Then she said, 'I'm sorry. We need Sarah here.'

Sarah turned to matron, 'The Red Cross are starting the search for missing people, aren't they?' She went over to the woman at the window. 'They need me here. But I can keep a lookout for your daughter. I can ask more people here in the city whether they've seen her. My father's helping at other hospitals. I can ask him.'

The woman nodded. 'You are so like her. A different hair colour—hers is fair where your hair is dark. But she's the only one I have left now. Please help me to find her.'

'Have the police . . . ?' Matron stood up from behind her table.

The woman picked up her gloves and umbrella. 'The police went into hiding, they say. There were no laws last week. And they won't want to help me.' She twisted the pale lace gloves into a tight fist. 'I'd be looking for my husband as well, only I've been told they've taken him off to an English prison. That's what people say, but no one can tell me for sure. His division was one of the last to surrender, in the Jacob's factory.'

Sarah didn't understand. She didn't believe what she was hearing. Hadn't this well-dressed American woman just told them her husband was one of the rebels? And she was bold enough to talk about it to people she hardly knew. What were Americans doing, fighting with the rebels? How could she be proud of what had happened? And how could she be so calm when everyone said all the rebels were going to be shot?

'Please will you help me find my daughter, Sarah? Her name is Daisy, but heaven knows what name she called herself by once she walked out of that school of hers. She was supposed to be safe in school and all I know for certain is that she walked out of there on Easter Monday and went to the post office. One of the telegram women saw her there.'

Sarah still couldn't understand how an American could have got involved with the group of Irish rebels fighting the British army.

'So was she taken prisoner by the rebels?'

Mrs Healey shook her head. 'They wouldn't have needed to make her a prisoner. I was going to take her out of the city that Monday morning, but she didn't know I was coming to get her. She was always a rebel. She knew her father wanted the Irish to fight against the British. That would have been enough for her.'

Sarah got up and went to the door and then walked back again. She had seen the GPO that morning. If the woman's daughter had stayed in there with the rebels, she was bound to be a prisoner by now if she wasn't somewhere in a hospital.

'I'm sorry for you that they all surrendered,' she said.

She didn't care any longer what matron thought of her, what anyone thought of her. She didn't know what she thought of the rebels any longer, with all the stories of executions, but she knew she couldn't hate them. She knew it wasn't right to shoot them after they had given themselves up and handed over their weapons.

'I wanted the fighting to end, but now I wish the rebels had carried on. Now that the British army are just going to shoot them.'

She saw the shocked faces of the two women, but nothing could stop her anger. 'Haven't you heard? The British soldiers have started shooting all the rebels! Some people say they're even shooting women and girls. Nobody knows what they're going to do any more.'

Matron stood up. 'Be careful what you're saying,

Sarah. You don't know what people are thinking. You have to be careful. These are dangerous times.'

But she didn't say any more about it, not then or even weeks afterwards when the British questioned her about rebel sympathizers among the nurses.

Outside a steady rain threw water on the bloodstained cobbles.

Sarah walked with Mrs Healey through the castle yard and over to the main gates. 'I wish I could help you, but I don't even know what Daisy looks like,' she said. 'She's the same age as me—so that means she'll be nearly fourteen. You say she looks like me, but will people know who I'm talking about if I just say she looks like me?'

'You tell them she has silver-blonde hair and she looks just like you.'

Mrs Healey gave Sarah her umbrella while she opened her handbag. Inside the elegant card folder of a Boston photographic studio were the photographs which had been posted to them in Ireland during the month before Easter. The one of Daisy showed a girl with a face like Sarah's, but with her mother's silver-blonde hair, cascading in curls over the shoulder of a white dress. There was another photograph of Daisy with her parents, in the same studio. Mrs Healey gave Sarah the one of Daisy on her own.

'Show this to as many people as you can. Tell people about her.'

She stared at the picture and held on to Sarah's hand. 'She's nearly as beautiful as you.' Then she kissed Sarah on the cheek and held both her shoulders as she said goodbye. 'Be very careful, Sarah,' she said. 'Be careful. Everything's changed now. Dublin isn't the city it used to be. Be careful.' She gave Sarah an envelope with an address in the suburbs outside Dublin. 'The people at this address will tell you where to find me.'

She walked away from the castle gate without looking back. The rain bounced off the cobbles and then hissed back at them and ran along the cracks, scouring the pavements outside, brightening up the grey sky. There was a roll of thunder and lightning flashed and people sprinted across the yard, racing the rain. The pavements were being scrubbed clean. The air was bright with the relief that comes when a storm finally breaks.

Sarah smiled as she walked back into her ward, pretending to brush waves of water off her sleeves. Her first thought when she had been called to matron's rooms was that her father must have finally come to take her home. But she had a job to do before she left Dublin. The photograph of Daisy was tucked inside her belt underneath her apron. She had taken one look at the girl as she climbed up the stairs and then put the picture away carefully. It was only at the end of her duty, when she and Kitty had finished washing the supper dishes and were just about to go round the ward with thermometers, that she took the photo out.

'This is the American girl I told you about—the one who's missing.'

Kitty opened the cardboard folder. 'They're right. She does look just like you. Except for the hair. Fancy having hair that colour! Like a fillum star.'

'That's like her mother. Very fine. You should have seen her. Of course, they're American.' Sarah was proud of the beautiful picture, because people said the girl looked like her. She wanted to help in the search, to be the one to find the American girl. 'It looks like they use some strange American hair dye at first—but her mother's hair really is that colour.' The girl, Daisy, looked like an actress, in that bright, white dress, with the archway behind her in the photograph, covered in roses.

'But she does look like you,' Kitty said. 'What colour eyes?'

Sarah shrugged. 'I don't know. I've never met her.' Both girls peered at the photograph and then Kitty looked into Sarah's eyes. 'Brown like yours. No, blue—that goes better with blonde hair. What do you think?'

Sarah wasn't allowed to say what she thought, as the ward sister arrived to see what had happened to the thermometers.

As the night duty staff arrived, Sarah was sitting down next to the young Sinn Feiner, who had had his eyes open again that afternoon. The ward sister encouraged them to talk to the men, even the ones who couldn't reply.

'The hearing is the last thing to go, you know, when they're dying,' matron had said. 'It still does them a power of good to talk to them.'

So Sarah talked to the boy whenever his eyes were open and she thought he was awake—about the city and the sights she had seen as she walked back into the city from home. When she ran out of things to say, she talked to him about the weather, so that she was glad of the thunderstorm that day. It gave her more to talk about. When she talked about the torrential rain, she pointed to the long, high windows, where the rain was still trickling down even now, several hours after the worst of the storm had gone. He didn't turn his head to the window when she pointed, but she was used to that. Matron had explained, 'Even when their eyes are open, it doesn't mean they can actually see anything.'

But there was something different. His eyes were open as they had been once or twice a day—but this time they were not just fixed, unseeing, Sarah realized in an instant. If he didn't look at the window, it wasn't because he couldn't see the window, it was because he

126

was looking at her. Staring at her. She moved her face away from him and over to the left and he followed her with his eyes. She stood up and walked around to the other side of his bed. His eyes moved slightly, so that he could see her.

She opened the screens on the ward side of his bed and got Kitty's attention.

'Look, we can leave the screens off now. Tell sister.' She folded the second screen flat against the wall. 'He's getting better. He follows you with his eyes. Look.'

Sister Dawson walked over to their end of the room, to see what was happening, and the tall young soldier they called Michael followed after her from the far end of the ward.

'This laddy could do with going home, couldn't you, Michael?' the sister laughed. 'If only we knew where we could send him to. He'll always have a limp, but he's not that sick that he needs a bed any longer. Only in his mind. We can't get him to go to bed after all that thunder. But he's the best ward helper we've had, aren't you, now?' She laughed again. 'It's true. Can you get me a chair, Michael, while I sit down and have a long talk with your man here.' She shook her head as she leaned over the young boy again. 'Will you look at what they've done to his face?' she said. 'It's a crime.'

She took down the thermometer. 'Sending them out to fight at that age. I wish we knew his name.' Then she raised her voice. 'Can you see me, young man?' The soldier looked straight at her. She moved her head to the right and his eyes followed her to where Sarah was standing beside her. The sister moved again and this time the soldier didn't follow her with his eyes. He stared at Sarah.

'Well, I can tell who his sweetheart is.'

The sister nudged Kitty. 'Will you just look at that?'

Then she turned round. 'Well, here's Michael with my chair at last. I'll just sit here for a while and have a talk with our laddy here. You run along, now, you two. You need to go off duty now. Thank you, Michael.' She nodded at the young soldier. 'You'll be needing to get into your own bed now. You need all the sleep you can get.'

But the tall young soldier didn't go off to his bed. Sarah and Kitty turned and watched him, as they were about to go off to the nurse's supper room. He walked right up to the young Sinn Feiner and stood there staring at him. Then he said the same thing again and again. Over and over again, sometimes as if he were absolutely certain what he was talking about, sometimes as a question, he said the same word. 'Michael?'

He reached out and stroked the boy's head and then held his hand and kissed it, crying. Then he moved to the opposite side of the bed and grabbed the soldier's hand again, shouting out, 'He'll be all right, won't he, sister? The doctors will take care of him. You'll be all right now, Michael. They'll look after you in here.'

'Now he's gone completely out of his mind.'

Kitty moved forwards to try and get him back to bed, but Sister Dawson waved her away.

'You get off and get some rest, you two. He's harmless enough. We'll get him to his own bed as soon as we're done here.' She shook her head. 'It won't be long now.'

11

The sun shook them awake next morning, in the long, crowded room where the extra nurses and helpers had found places to sleep. It was a beautiful day. No one could talk about the world getting back to normal; the world had changed too much in that week for things ever to be the same again. But it was a beautiful day, the sort of day when everything in the world looks better.

The men were still sleeping or lying quietly as Sarah and Kitty arrived on their ward. The sunlight streamed through the windows and Sarah walked down the narrow rows in between the extra beds to get to the end near the sister's table. The screens were around the young Sinn Feiner's bed again and Sarah took hold of one to move it aside. Sister Dawson stood up and shook her head, so that Sarah left the screen and went over to her table.

'He died a short time ago.'

She took hold of Sarah's hand and whispered. 'It did him good, all the time you spent talking to him.' She made Sarah sit down. 'And there are miracles, even in times like this. Would you believe he had his brother with him at the end?'

She took Sarah over to the curtained bed, quietly drew the screen aside and closed it behind them. A soldier was sitting beside the bed weeping; the tall young soldier they knew as Michael.

'We know their names now at last. Both of them.' The ward sister put her hand on his shoulder. 'This is Diarmid, after all. Whenever he called out the name of

Michael, he was talking about his brother, the young laddy who was lying here. I'm so sorry we couldn't save him.'

Sarah said nothing. Fear thumped her in the stomach. She looked towards the bed again where Diarmid sat, holding his brother's hand, staring at his face. Sarah wanted to cry, as she had cried so often during that week—but she didn't want to tear aside the curtain of silence around the two brothers. She stood beside Diarmid, clenching and unclenching her hands, then rocking backwards and forwards on her heels, telling herself she was not going to cry, stopping the tears so that the pain gathered just behind her eyes.

Diarmid looked up at her. 'Tell me he wasn't a soldier for the British army. I don't believe that story they told about him.'

Sarah shook her head and he turned to look back at his brother.

'My brother would never have fought for the British army.' There was a long silence, before Diarmid spoke again, still looking at Michael. 'The British could have had me out there fighting last week. Killing my own brother. If I hadn't been wounded and in here, I could have fired the bullets that killed Michael. Without even knowing what or who I was shooting at.'

It was the first time Sarah had heard Diarmid speaking clearly, slowly emerging from the nightmare that had started out in the trenches in France.

He turned and looked at Sarah. 'They won't get me shooting for them again. I won't be part of an army that kills the Irish.'

The next day, with a map of Ireland spread out on the huge table in the centre of the ward, they managed to locate the district the two brothers came from, farming just outside Dublin.

Sarah was allowed to go to the farm with Sister Dawson and a driver. The ruins of Dublin were still smouldering, people standing around staring as buildings were ripped down by heavy machinery. Each time they got to a checkpoint, the hospital driver told the soldiers on duty how glad he was to have the thick tyres on the military vehicle they were using. Then they carried on, bumping over roads still littered with broken glass and bricks. Out in the country the roads were clearer, but so narrow that when they got nearer to the farm they had to stop and ask the way four times.

'Will we leave this great big tank outside, away from the farm?' Sister Dawson said. 'We don't want to scare his mother and father.'

A black and white collie rushed out to greet them, wildly wagging her tail. Then an old, black labrador ambled round the corner from the farmyard to the front gate and sat down in front of the gate, panting and drumming his tail on the ground. Sarah calmed the young dog down, talking to her and stroking the older one.

'That's a jolly pair of old dogs, right enough.' Sister Dawson carefully opened and closed the gate around them while the driver stayed with the truck outside. The yard was quiet. It was almost twelve o'clock. Even the dogs were quiet now. The two of them walked across the quiet yard, almost wanting to go on tiptoes across the stones to stop the gravel crunching as they walked.

The long, cream-washed farmhouse with red-painted windows stood in the shade, so that the woman who opened the door squinted into the sun. Then she saw the Red Cross armband on Sarah's sleeve.

'I know the truth of it already.' She turned to go back into the house. 'Thank you very much for coming, but you won't be needing to tell me any more.' Sister Dawson

131

and Sarah were left standing on the doorstep as she disappeared down the narrow, dark corridor towards the back of the house.

They knocked at the door again and waited. The black labrador settled himself in the shade on the doorstep, his tail thumping against the cold slate floor. The collie scampered silently through to the back of the house, as if even she had learned to show silent respect for the feelings of the people inside.

Then a man came towards them from across the yard. He looked older than the woman, with a black waistcoat over his striped, collarless shirt. He took the watch out of his waistcoat pocket. 'She won't be answering your knocking now,' he said. 'The Angelus. She'll be saying her prayers for our two boys.' He took a big handkerchief out of his trouser pocket and blew his nose. 'One of them dead and one of them missing so long she has to believe he's dead. Both of them too young to go fighting.'

Then he looked straight at Sarah's armband, noticing it for the first time. 'And if you're from the British to tell her for certain that Diarmid's killed as well—'

'He's not dead.' Sarah stepped forward, interrupting him.

'I'm so sorry to bring you the news, sir,' said Sister Dawson. 'Michael was too badly wounded. He passed away yesterday morning in Dublin Castle. But Diarmid is alive. That's why we've come to see you.'

'Alive?'

'Alive and out of danger. In the hospital in Dublin Castle.'

They followed him through to the back of the house, to the dark, cool kitchen, where his wife sat with her back to them, staring out to the fields beyond. He put his hand on her shoulder. 'Diarmid is alive, Mary.'

Then he sat down beside her, with his arm around her shoulder and both of them wept. Sarah and Sister

Dawson moved backwards slowly and then made their way out to the front of the house, where Sarah sat herself down on the step next to the black labrador. Sister Dawson went out of the yard to tell the driver they would have to wait, then sat down beside Sarah. Time passed. The flies buzzed around the old, black dog and his tail thumped harder. The young collie jumped around Sarah and licked her face.

Then the farmer came and took them back into the kitchen, where Michael's mother was brewing up tea.

'I thought Diarmid was dead as well. I thought I'd lost the two of them and never a grave to lay flowers.' She pulled a picture of Michael and Diarmid from the mantelpiece, a picture taken in a Dublin studio seven years before when Michael had done his first holy communion. 'I thought my two sons were dead and now one of them is come back to me.' She crossed herself and started to cry again.

'Look, they told me Michael was dead.' And she took out a carefully flattened, bloodstained piece of paper with torn edges from the pages of her Bible. 'They brought me this letter from him. It's in Michael's hand, and it says if I'm reading it he's probably dead.' Sarah looked over Sister Dawson's shoulder, as they read the letter Michael had written while he was still in the GPO.

'They told me the post office was all burnt out,' she said and then she cried again. 'Oh, I didn't sleep when I thought of my Mikey being burnt to death. But you say he was still alive when he came to you?'

'He had two bad shot wounds. He was very badly hurt. But he wasn't conscious. He didn't have any pain.' Sarah looked at the letter over the ward sister's shoulder.

'They operated and he started to come awake.' Sister Dawson folded the letter and gave it back.

133

Then Sarah said, 'Who brought you the letter from Michael?'

Michael's mother looked to her husband. 'It was one of the Volunteers. Two young women who escaped out of the city. They won't want us giving their whereabouts to the British army.'

'We are not the British army.' Sister Dawson stood up. 'And I am not British, thank you very much. I'm an Irish nurse and proud to be Irish.'

Michael's father handed her a cup of tea. 'No insult intended, young lady.' He pulled out her chair again to get her to sit down. 'It's just, they're right to be careful at a time like this.' He nodded with his head in the general direction of Dublin. 'They say the British army are shooting anyone they think might have anything to do with it. They'll be coming for me in the end, I reckon. Once they start to think that Mikey couldn't have got the ideas he had without me putting them in his head. Which I didn't.'

He sipped his own tea. 'Which is not to say I don't agree there should be freedom for Ireland and we should have our own government.' He nodded to his wife. 'It's just I think there's fighting enough going on, in France and Belgium. And fighting never solves anything.'

'If we could speak to the Volunteers who brought the letter, we might be able to trace some other people,' Sarah said. 'Michael was carrying a diary for someone else, but we don't know who it was yet.' Michael's father nodded to his wife to get a pencil and paper and she went into the parlour towards the front of the house.

'And they might be able to help another family as well.'

Sarah pulled out the photograph of Daisy which she carried in her dress pocket, under her apron. Daisy's mother had been certain she had got herself involved with the Volunteers.

'Was this one of the young women who came to you with the letter?'

Michael's mother came back into the room. She looked at the photograph and shook her head. 'I'd have remembered a young girl as beautiful as that.' Then she looked at Sarah. 'My, but she's the image of you. Except that you've got your lovely black curls and she's all blonde like a fillum star.'

Sarah put the photograph away. She had seen some of the women Volunteers, very serious young women in their green uniforms. It wasn't possible that a girl as pretty as Daisy could have been part of their army. She thought it was most likely that Daisy had found shelter and was trying now to make her way back to her school, and being held back at barricades and sent back to the house where she had found shelter in the first place, like thousands of other people who were being prevented from moving about their business in Dublin by the barricades and suspicious soldiers on every street corner.

While they finished their tea, Michael's father wrote an address down on the piece of paper and then ripped it up into tiny pieces. 'No, I can't give you that. It's not safe,' he said. 'Not safe for any of the Volunteers at the moment.' Then he put his hat on. 'I'll take you to visit the ones who came here.'

They walked out of the back of the yard, through a small gate and across a field. After the third field, he said to Sarah, 'It's better if just one of you comes with me.' And they left Sister Dawson sitting on a stile. He walked too quickly for Sarah to be afraid. She wasn't even afraid when he told her to put her apron over her head as they approached the house, so that she had no idea what the front of the house looked like.

135

Inside, the thickness of the walls showed in the deep recesses of all the windows, where the light from outside bounced on the pale wooden shutters and sprang back into the rooms. They sat and waited in the huge drawing room. Two women came in, smiling. One of them was a girl of about sixteen. The other was obviously her mother.

'We hear you've brought us wonderful news—that one of our young Irishmen was not killed as we thought. Thank you for coming to tell his parents so soon. Will you have some tea?'

Sarah shook her head. She couldn't find the normal, polite words she knew she should use. Who were these tall, elegant women with the accents of English ladies? Michael's father explained that they had just had tea. The grandfather clock in the corner made little holes in the silence, like pins in a pincushion. The older woman stared at Sarah and then out of the deep window to the bright daylight outside. Sarah looked around the beautifully furnished room, with paintings on the panelled wall between each of the windows. It was much grander than her parents' house. At the end of the room, the polished black of a grand piano sparkled in the sunlight.

After a long time, Michael's father spoke, 'It's just, we wanted to ask, how did you get hold of the letter to tell us Mikey was dead? Did one of you see him being shot down?'

The older woman shook her head. 'We had these arrangements. We carried letters for one another. A young girl, one of the Volunteers, had Michael's letter on her when she was wounded. We thought, if she had it, it meant for certain he was dead. The GPO was totally destroyed in the flames.'

She looked at Sarah again and frowned.

'It was a bad business altogether.' Michael's father,

with his hat in his hand, looked uncomfortable perched on the edge of the deep cushions of one of the sofas dotted about the long room. 'Shooting at women and girls and boys as young as Michael.'

'All of them fighting for their country,' the woman said. 'We'll have some tea sent in, shall we?' She nodded to her daughter and then moved so that the sun was behind her and looked at Sarah again.

'But did they really shoot at young girls? Did they really have girls doing the shooting?' asked Sarah.

She had heard so many different rumours. And the newspapers didn't tell you what had happened. After her whole week in the castle being surrounded by shooting and corridors full of the wounded and dying, the newspaper report had merely stated, 'There was a faint-hearted attack on Dublin Castle, which resulted in the shooting of one policeman.'

That was all. Nothing about the night after night of shooting. Nothing about the lack of food and medicine for pain relief. Nothing about the hurried midnight burials of nameless soldiers. The newspapers wouldn't tell you the truth. If you wanted to know the truth, you had to go out and look for it yourself. Which was why she knew she had to ask more of this woman Volunteer, this wealthy woman who obviously thought there was something wonderful about young girls and boys getting themselves shot, as long as they got themselves killed for Ireland.

Sarah was angry. She wanted to take the older woman by the hand and force her to witness some of the sights she had seen in the hospital during Easter week. Force her to walk through the corridors running with the blood of the soldiers from both sides lying on tarpaulins on the floor. Force her to see some of the men with their faces blown to bits. She wanted to hit the woman whose name she would never get to know, for thinking that rows of dying and wounded men and women was something wonderful as long as they were dying for Ireland.

The woman looked straight at Sarah.

'The girl who was carrying the letter about Michael was a very special Volunteer. One of our comrades from overseas.' She looked quickly at Sarah. 'Very like you in appearance. You must forgive me for looking at you so closely, but she really was very like you, and quite a young girl, really. Just your age, I'd guess. She was in the group of women helping to evacuate the wounded from the GPO in the final hours when the whole of the front had gone up in flames.'

She stopped talking and listened. The panelled wooden wall behind her suddenly revealed a door and a servant arrived pushing a tea trolley, with the woman's daughter behind him. He moved the trolley over to the group of chairs where they were sitting, served out tea, and then disappeared the same way he had come, through the almost invisible door in the wood-panelled wall.

Sarah didn't want the woman's tea. She didn't want the ceremony of milk and sugar, of tiny cakes being offered round on tiny china plates. She didn't want anything to do with this woman with her English accent, with her talk about Volunteers dying for a glorious end while she sat in her drawing room sipping tea. She wanted to know what had happened to Daisy Healey. Because she was sure it was Daisy the woman was talking about.

'What was her name? The young girl who gave you the letter?'

'We don't ask names—unless we need to inform next-of-kin. We just act as messengers.'

'So she isn't dead?'

'She was badly wounded. But we have no further information.'

'How was she wounded? What happened? I thought

she was in the group helping to get the wounded out of the building. How could they have shot at her?'

The woman put her cup and saucer carefully down on the trolley. Then she held out her hand for Sarah's cup. 'May I? Another cup of tea?'

When Sarah shook her head she answered, 'You mustn't think I was there, my dear. In the GPO. They would have had me in prison in England by now if I had been. No, I was just visiting the sick and wounded, in the Jervis Street hospital. I'm afraid I know little of the events of that night. All I know is that there was a young girl in the hospital—American, I think, who asked for a letter to be passed on. And that's what I did. Since that time it has not been safe in Dublin for Volunteers like us.'

Sarah stood up. Michael's father put his cup and saucer on the trolley and picked his cap off the floor next to the sofa.

'But she might still be alive? In Jervis Street? In the hospital?'

The woman stroked the long pearl necklace that hung almost to her waist and pulled at the beads, as if each of them needed polishing. 'I wouldn't like to raise your hopes, my dear. She was very badly wounded.' Then she stood up, followed by her daughter. 'It was last Monday I visited. Very soon after the ceasefire. No, it's more than a week ago now. So much has happened since then. I haven't been back. Dublin is far too dangerous at the moment.'

12

'When can you go? Why don't you go right away this evening? Matron won't mind. She was there when you said you would help Daisy's mother to look for her.'

On the way back into Dublin, Sarah and Sister Dawson huddled together for warmth. It was May 11th, and the evening air was cold and damp.

'They won't let me in. You should know what hospitals are like.'

Sarah tried to warm herself by pulling her sleeves right down over her hands, but the cold air whistled through the sides of the truck, jolting them over the rubble-strewn cobbles. The gun-grey sky glinted after the rain they had had just outside the city.

'It's getting too late now. And we're supposed to be going on night duty. And they might not let anyone near her if she's a rebel,' said Sarah.

'Don't talk like that! They can't treat her like a dangerous rebel, a girl as young as you are.'

'Well that's what she is. She was fighting with the rebels, wasn't she?'

'What must her parents feel?'

'Her father's a Sinn Feiner as well, isn't he? Maybe it's true what they say about people in America working for the rebels,' said Sarah.

'Sh! Don't talk like that. You never know who's listening.'

Sister Dawson motioned to the driver in the front of

140

the truck. The engine was very loud, so loud that he sometimes wore ear protectors. He wasn't wearing them for the drive back to Dublin and they had had to shout when they wanted to say anything to him. He was an Irish driver, not part of the British army, but you had to be careful.

'I'll go to Jervis Street in the morning, as soon as we finish on night duty.'

Back at the castle, soldiers crowded round to help the two nurses down from the high steps of the armoured truck. The castle yard was already dark, with a watchfire burning in one corner. Everything was peaceful. Sarah was glad to be back there, to another cheerful policeman calling out that they were his angels of mercy, as he did every time he saw them, to the cool, dark corridors and the bright, clean wards.

When they went on duty, the ward lamps were already dimmed and the men were settled in their beds.

Sarah fought to keep herself awake that night. She hadn't had the sleep they were supposed to take before they went on night duty. So she walked around the ward. Every time her legs and arms started to itch and shake with tiredness and she felt her eyes closing, she shook herself, got up and walked around.

Diarmid wasn't asleep, but he was quiet. Sarah crept over to him and told him about her visit to his parents and how they would be coming to take him home. Sister Dawson came and stood next to her. 'It looks as if you'll sleep now, young man,' she said. 'And you, young lady. Come and have your tea.'

It was midnight. Sarah had travelled far that day. She had found two brothers serving as soldiers on either side of the Irish rebellion not knowing they could be forced to fight each other. She had visited Michael and Diarmid's parents with news of life and death. She was sure she would hear good news about Daisy now. It wasn't possible that Daisy was dead. There had been too many deaths already, too much sadness and confusion. Sarah wanted peace.

That day she had met Irish landed families, rich and poor, living close to each other but worlds apart. She had travelled between different worlds, between the devastation and ruins in Dublin and the joy of spring in the countryside. She had seen Michael's parents move from total despair to hope. And now she had come home again, back to her work, away from the struggling world outside and back to the work of putting people back together.

Michael was dead, but she had seen other wounded men like him journey from certain death to recovery. She felt certain now that Daisy was recovering too, that the whole of the city would slowly start to mend. She trailed back in her tired mind over the week of the fighting. Either the men they took in had died the night they arrived or somehow they had got through. And the woman they had visited that afternoon had seen Daisy several days after she would have been wounded. There was every reason to believe she would be sitting up in bed talking by now.

An ambulance drew up in the yard down below. The nurses put their cups down.

'A strange time for new arrivals. Shall we go and have a look?'

The ward sister looked quickly up and down the rows of sleeping men.

'Two minutes won't hurt.'

Sarah and Kitty climbed on stools in the supper room kitchen.

'They don't look sick at all.' Sarah leaned even further out of the window. In the darkness she could make out an officer, holding out an arm to steady a woman stepping down from the motor ambulance. The woman pushed his arm away. Sarah could see she wasn't the one who was sick, striding away from the officer across the yard and towards the entrance. The other, younger woman who followed them out into the yard also refused his help.

'That'll be General Connolly's wife.' Sister Dawson crossed herself.

Sarah turned away from the window for a second. 'Why? Has he taken ill again? They said he was wounded in the leg. Why are they here in the middle of the night?'

'You go and have a look. See if you can find out. I'll stay here.'

Sarah got down from the stool and smoothed down her skirt.

'Go on. You'll need to be quick.'

Kitty stayed at the window. 'Run along. See what you can find out.'

Sarah knew where they had the room for General Connolly. It wasn't difficult to find. Ever since he had been brought to the castle on the night of the surrender, they had had at least ten soldiers on duty outside, when the man was so badly wounded he could scarcely sit up without help, let alone escape from the heavily guarded castle. There were now even more soldiers stationed all along the corridor. It was hard to tell what was happening, but there was an awful lot of noise. New soldiers came and went. Officers shouted out orders.

A young woman still wearing her hat and coat came out of Connolly's room. She walked straight over to Sarah, cutting through the group of British soldiers as if they didn't exist. She held herself straight and strong as she walked, not looking at any of them.

'Can I sit with you, nurse? My mother is with him.'

The soldiers moved aside. There was a kitchen near

the room they had put the general in, like the kitchen for the wards upstairs, and Sarah took the young woman in there.

'Thank you.' She sat down on the stool Sarah had offered her, took her hat off and put it on the table. 'You have all been very good to him. The nurses and doctors here in the hospital. But I can't talk to them. I can't look at them.' She nodded towards the British soldiers outside the open door.

Sarah was wide awake now. She moved the kettle sideways on the range where it was always left, simmering away.

'I can make you some tea, if you like.'

The girl shook her head. 'I may have to go back in, if he needs me.'

She looked as if she had been crying, but her face was fixed and determined. 'I won't cry any more.' She looked straight at Sarah. 'I won't let them see me cry.' She took her gloves off and laid them next to her hat. Her hands, her long, elegant fingers turned into fists, pressed hard against the table so that the knuckles turned white.

'They woke him up at eleven and told him he was to die at dawn. Then they sent the ambulance for us. But I won't let them see me cry.'

A soldier stood at the kitchen door. 'He needs to see you again, miss.'

General Connolly's daughter put her gloves on again, slowly, and placed her hat on her head. She turned to Sarah and smiled. 'Is my hat right?'

Sarah nodded and followed her through the group of soldiers to the door of the room. Another nurse already there, attending to Connolly who was still so weak he could only lift his head and shoulders from the bed. Sarah was just about to go, but the general's daughter turned and looked at her. Nobody was forcing Sarah to move, so she stayed.

The girl's mother was sitting beside her husband, looking as if she were about to faint. After a short time the officer said, 'It will soon be time, Mrs Connolly.'

The injured man turned his head to say goodbye to his wife, and she fell across his bed in tears. Sarah and the other nurse and two soldiers had to half carry, half walk her out of the room, leaving her daughter behind.

She came and joined them a few minutes later, in the room where they had taken her mother to recover. Mrs Connolly was crying, but her daughter was calm and strong.

'What will happen now?' Sarah sat beside the girl, urging her to take a drink of water, but she refused everything.

The girl stood up and walked away from the bed in the nurse's rooms, where her mother was lying on her side, facing the wall. She whispered, watching her mother all the time, making sure she couldn't hear what they were saying. 'I suppose they will shoot him.'

'But they can't.' Sarah felt again as if she was travelling in a foreign country, a place where she knew none of the rules. 'He's a sick man. He can't sit up. How can they shoot him? How can they?'

The girl shook her head and whispered again. 'I am not going to cry. I have promised my father. I am not going to let them see me crying. You mustn't ask me these questions.'

'I'll come back again soon.'

Sarah dashed up the stairs again to her own ward duty, to see if she was needed. In the whole of the long, silent ward, only one lamp was burning, at the table where Sister Dawson was sitting, writing in the log. Everything was peaceful, so quiet she could hear the men breathing. The scenes she had just witnessed, the arrival of the ambulance in the yard, the soldiers milling around in the corridor, the sobbing wife, the strong, calm girl, smoothing the gloves on to her elegant hands while they discussed the best way to shoot her father, they were scenes from a different world.

She told her story quickly and Sister Dawson sent her away again, to help out where she was most needed. But by the time she got back to where she had left Connolly's daughter and his wife they had gone. The nurse was folding up the blanket they had used to cover Connolly's wife.

'I can't believe they're going to do it.'

She put the grey blanket down at the end of the bed. 'They wouldn't shoot a wounded man, now, would they? That's what I told his wife. They've made a mistake, most likely. And he's such a gentleman. You couldn't hope to meet a nicer gentleman.'

They went out into the corridor leading from the nurse's kitchen to Connolly's room. After the weeks of the corridors and staircases being filled with British soldiers, the emptiness was cold and threatening. 'They've taken him away right enough. On a stretcher. And they had the priest here as soon as his wife had gone.'

She tried the door of the room where Connolly had been for the last week, but it was locked.

'They'll have made a mistake,' Sarah said. 'They wouldn't shoot a wounded man.'

146

13

There was no escape. The headlines flew at her like a sniper's bullets.

EXECUTION OF JAMES CONNOLLY
JAMES CONNOLLY SHOT THIS MORNING

Sarah had not slept. The minute her duty finished she had decided to make her way to the hospital in Jervis Street to see if she could find Daisy Healey, to see if she could make something good come out of all the madness. The newspaper headlines lay in wait to ambush her.

She closed her eyes at the blackened letters firing pain. She dodged and moved as quickly as she could past the newspaper stands, past news boys crying out the words. She had seen death in the weeks since she had started her training. She had seen death even though her mother had tried to stop her being a nurse because she was too young to see people die. She had seen dreadful wounds and men released from their pain by death.

But this was murder.

She had seen James Connolly alive the night before, propped up on pillows when his wife and daughter came to see him because he could not sit without help. She had seen the ambulance that came to collect him. She had been settling in to the peace, the quiet, and the healing calm of the hospital after the horrors of the week before. She had started to feel safe, now that everything was over and even the very seriously wounded were recovering. She had grown confident that she would find

Daisy Healey recovering in hospital and that life in Dublin would slowly return to normal.

But the thought of that ambulance, with a nurse and doctor inside to look after their patient, an ambulance driving an injured man off in the dark to be shot at first light opened up a gaping hole in her world, threw everything into terror and confusion, like an unexploded landmine years after a war is over. She sat down. She had to sit down on the edge of the pavement. The world whirled and flew around her, with crackling lights in the darkness and people moving strangely like the figures in a silent film. She knew she was going to faint, and put her head down on her knees to shut out the swimming, tumbling world. Voices grabbed at her, pulling her up out of the darkness, asking her if she was all right and she nodded, not speaking in case she was sick. She was still wearing her nurse's uniform, so they took her to the place they thought she had come from—to the Jervis Street Hospital.

Sarah had not seen any wounded children during the week of fighting and very few women had been brought to the Castle Hospital. But as she sat in the receiving area at Jervis Street and slowly felt the life coming back into her weak arms and legs, men, women, and children came in and out of the department where she was sitting, all of them with horrific wounds and stories of their experiences during the last week. They had been shot at by the British who thought they were rebels. Their houses had been raided by the British searching for rebels. They had been shot at by the Volunteers while they were shooting at the British. In the war that had raged in the middle of their city there were far more civilians killed and wounded than there were military on either side.

It was after midday when Sarah was allowed to go up to the ward where the women Volunteers from the

Republican army had been taken. Soldiers were standing outside, two on each side of the door. There were so many wounded that the normal beds had low camp beds set up between them, and Sarah made her way down the crowded rows looking into the faces of any of the women and girls whose faces she could see. She got to the end of the row, where the ward sister had her little office.

'I'm sorry. I must be in the wrong ward.' She stood just at the edge of the glass door, waiting for the sister to look up from her writing.

'Who are you looking for?'

'They told me this was the ward for the women Volunteers. Someone said a girl I am helping to look for might be in here. From America.' Sarah gave her the name.

The ward sister looked through her list of names. 'No Americans here now, my dear. No one of that name. Not here.' Then she looked at Sarah and pointed to her uniform. 'How are you involved with any of them? You're not one of the Sinn Feiners, now are you?' Sarah shook her head and the ward sister frowned. 'She wouldn't have blonde hair, now would she? Long, silver-blonde hair like a fillum star? Someone said *she* was American. But she wasn't doing any talking.'

'Was she here?'

The sister shook her head at the waste of another young life. 'She looked so like you, now I look at you properly. Sit down, my dear.' She closed the glass door and made Sarah sit on the swivel chair next to her desk. 'I'm afraid she died two days after they brought her in.' She opened her logbook, rustled through the pages and pointed to the name. 'We had a different surname for her, but I wouldn't blame anyone for getting the wrong name, with the dead and dying all around you like they were last week.' She saw Sarah peering over the desk at the logbook and laid her hand over both pages. 'I'm sure about her first name, though. Someone said her name was Daisy.'

Sarah nodded. She was moving slowly, like a circus tightrope walker keeping her balance. Like General Connolly's daughter. Keeping control of her feelings. Knowing that keeping control was important to survival.

The ward sister ran her fingers over the brief entry in the logbook. 'She was so badly wounded. Hit in the chest. It was only a matter of time. It says here she was carrying a letter, which she wanted handed out to a visitor. But there was nothing else. The letter must have been sent off.'

A nurse came in to ask the ward sister for help and she rushed out, closing the door quietly behind her. Sarah could see everything in the ward through the glass windows of the office and they could see her. So she didn't cry. She hit with her fists at the underneath of the desk, so no one would see her, to stop herself crying. She was angry at herself for even thinking of crying. She had never met this girl. What was Daisy to her anyway?

Sarah looked out at the nurses on the ward. No one was looking in to where she was sitting. She reached over and pulled the logbook towards her, carefully watching to make sure the sister couldn't see her. She found three entries about Daisy. The first one read, 'A group of Sinn Fein women. Number 5: Daisy, wounds to the chest and arms.'

The entry for the next day said that Daisy was conscious, but not speaking. A visitor had come, a woman saying she was Daisy's sister. That was where the false name had come from. The woman had taken the letter away. But there were other things. The third entry, the one which said she had died at 2.30 in the morning, listed her property. The logbook said 'Carrying a gun, in spite of her red-cross armband. Locket round her neck.' Sarah wanted to ask what had happened to the other things Daisy had been carrying or why she had been carrying a gun, or where she had got it from, but she knew she shouldn't have seen the logbook.

It didn't matter anyway. None of it mattered. What was the point of asking about a locket now Daisy was dead? And what was the point of crying? One more person dead, that was all. Hundreds of people had been killed in Dublin that week. Sarah stood up. Her face was fixed in an angry mask. She was angry with the men who had killed Daisy, angry with the British soldiers who had killed or wounded all five children of the couple she had met while she was waiting to go up to the ward. She was angry with herself for not finding Daisy alive. She had wanted so much to have good news for Daisy's mother. The only thing she could do now was to get back to her own hospital. But she wanted to tell people about it all, to tell someone. There had to be an end to all the killing.

She had almost got to the door of the ward when the sister caught up with her.

'You'll be wanting this.' She handed Sarah a small envelope marked with Daisy's name and the false surname. 'It's the locket she was wearing round her neck.'

'Can I ask,' Sarah lowered her voice to a whisper, 'where she is buried?'

The sister walked with her out into the corridor and continued to whisper. 'That I'm afraid I can't tell you, my dear.' She steered Sarah to the stairs. 'I don't think anyone can say for certain. There were so many people. The men were working night and day, even when it was dangerous. Some are buried in the churchyard down there. Some in the castle grounds, they say. They took them all over the place. I'm sure they'll have a list somewhere. For people to search for their lost loved ones when this is all over.'

There was nowhere to go after that. From the steps of the hospital, Sarah looked in three directions and sat for an hour, not knowing which way to go. She knew if she took the road to her left she could get to Henrietta Street and the parks and then just keep on walking along the road to the north out of the city for hours until she got home. They would send her back to school and she would try to forget. She could take the road to her right and walk quickly across the river and back to the hospital in the castle where she could forget herself in work.

But she stared ahead at the blackened ruins of the shop that had once stood at the corner of the road. She didn't know where to go or what to do. She took the locket out of her satchel, but she didn't open it. Then she put it away. She put her satchel over her shoulder, stood up and started to walk. Away from home. Away from the castle. Straight ahead and then along by the river, sometimes walking quickly, sometimes picking her way over broken glass and blackened wood. Past burnt-out carts and bicycles she walked for an hour, without being stopped at a barricade and without knowing where she was going.

A man on one corner was sweeping the pavement with a huge broom, acting as if he had all the time in the world. The clock on the wall behind him was still working, even though the closed door underneath it had a huge hole blown through, framing the blackened walls inside. It was the day they had shot General Connolly, propping him up to get a better shot at him on his stretcher, and the man sweeping the pavement was whistling, smiling and waving to Sarah as she walked past.

The Nelson Monument stood out to her right and the railway station loomed over on the other side of the river when Sarah walked into another barricade, soldiers stopping everyone who walked that way, making sure no one crossed the Heuston Bridge.

'Where are you heading for, miss? Have you got a pass for this way?'

Sarah looked at the young soldier who stood pointing his gun at her. She was still so angry she wanted to shout at him, 'I am trying to find the enemy. I want the shooting to stop.' But it wasn't his fault. He was just a young Irish man, doing his job with the British army. She showed him her pass for the castle.

'You can't cross the bridge down here with that, miss. You'll have to go back the way you came.' He lowered his gun as he lowered his voice, peering all around him as he spoke. 'There's too many people trying to get to Kilmainham Jail, miss, where they've had the executions. They're expecting trouble. We've got orders to keep this side clear. You'd best get yourself safely home.'

He wasn't the enemy, a young Irish soldier brought back from the war in France to fight a war in Ireland. Not unless her brother James was the enemy as well. But Connolly wasn't the enemy either, the man they had tied to his stretcher so he was sitting upright when they shot him. Sarah didn't know where to look any more for the enemy, or whatever it was that had torn her city to pieces. She turned and walked back quickly towards the centre of the ruined city.

14

Sarah shut the door quietly. She dragged a chair over towards the high shelf above the sink where she had left the little notebook to dry and then forgotten all about it. The May sunshine was dancing through the tall window, warming her as she reached over to the far right of the shelf. Sarah stood there for a long time, with the brittle, dry notebook in her hand, staring out of the window from where she balanced on the draining board, remembering all the times, night after night, when they had had to crawl past the windows on their hands and knees for fear of getting shot at.

She climbed down again, pulled her chair close to the window, and sat down, smoothing the wrinkled cover of the precious little book that she realized now must have belonged to some other soldier who had been fighting with Michael. It was obvious that many of the rebels had given a letter or a special keepsake for their parents to someone else who was fighting with them. She started to separate the pages, very carefully, easing apart the crinkled edges one by one without really reading them.

The very first page in the book was the hardest, stuck like glue to the endpaper of the little black book with its red spine. Sarah remembered the day she had frantically splashed the book with water, trying to wipe the blood and soot off everything she had taken out of the blood-soaked knapsack they had found with Michael. But she hadn't wanted to spoil the little book with too much water and there were bloodstains still, on the edges of every page, and blood that had spilled over or seeped inside, blotting out some of the words, draining the life away from them.

When her fingers had enough space to ease in between the first page and the endpaper, the work of laying open that first page moved faster until Sarah was finally able to read the name and address written on the front of the little book. There were two addresses. One was the convent school in Eccles Street. The other was an address in Boston, America.

Sarah sat back in the chair and sighed. Then she carefully put the book on the draining board under the window and put her head on her hands beside it. She wanted to cry, but there were no more tears. She wanted to cry, but didn't know why she should need to cry for a girl she had never met. She hadn't cried the day before, when she had walked for miles along by the Liffey after she found out that Daisy was dead. She had not cried when she saw other people sobbing and some of them screaming when they heard the news that Connolly had been executed. So many people had been killed in those few weeks, so many people that there were no more tears.

In her pocket, Sarah still had the photo Daisy's mother had given her, to help in her search. In an envelope from the hospital, she had the locket that had to go back to Daisy's parents. She put them both out on the draining board beside the book. She was not going to cry. Why should she cry about a girl she didn't even know?

She picked the book up and started to read, at the first entry, in March of that year. The whole book was in the form of a letter.

'Dear Mother and Father,
I never wished I had a sister until now. But there
are two Polish sisters in my dormitory who arrived here

a week before I did and they're evidently missing their
parents because they talk to each other non-stop in Polish
and cry and hug each other whenever they're alone.

Well, I don't have a sister. I just have this little
book to talk to, and I promised you I would write every
day, so I'll just imagine I am talking to you—or even
to my sister.

The Reverend Mother here tells everyone you have
both gone off to Paris and I can honestly say I don't
know where you are, though I hope you are both safe
and somewhere here in Ireland so you'll come back and
get me as soon as your important work is done.'

The whole of March, and the first three weeks of April,
told of Daisy's school life, how she was getting into
trouble for answering back or for not being tidy enough
or for running in the corridors. She liked the nuns and
they liked her. Some of them remembered teaching her
father's sister before the whole family moved to America
and the older nuns called her Mary because she reminded
them of her aunt. She liked the nuns but she missed her
parents and she wanted to get back home. Then, after days
and days of reading that not very much had happened
unless Daisy got herself into trouble, Sarah read the
longest entry Daisy had written, on the morning of April
24th. On that day, her sadness and loneliness cried out of
the pages until they gradually turned into a resolution to
actually do something, to get away from school for long
enough to send a telegram to Daisy's grandfather in
Boston.

There were five more pages of writing for that holiday
Monday, when Daisy slipped away from her school and
made her way to the post office, but those pages were
written at a furious pace, in rushed, scrawled handwriting,
from various places within the post office. And Daisy was

no longer sad. She was excited and hopeful. She wrote of the two flags flying high above the post office, the green, white, and gold flag and the green flag which said 'Irish Republic' on it. The pages and pages of writing made it sound as if nobody could have got much sleep, but there was a good ending to the day with the last thing Daisy wrote before she tried to sleep, *'At last I can be like the two of you and Grandpa. I can do something that I know would make you proud of me. I am doing something for Ireland.'*

On the back of the last page for the 24th, she had copied out the Proclamation to the People of Ireland, *'just in case I have to give away my last copy of the ones we were handing out. I know you will want to read it.'*

Sarah read the proclamation for only the second time,

> *'Irishmen and Irishwomen: In the name of God and of the dead generations from which she receives her old tradition of nationhood, Ireland, through us, summons her children to her flag and strikes for her freedom.'*

The first time Sarah had read the proclamation was out in the streets soon after the fighting had finished, with crowds of people standing round and jeering at the rebels who had been the cause of all their troubles that week. The words had a different ring to them now. It was right to talk of striking for freedom with the news of all the executions and the terrible things some of the British army had done to innocent civilians who had nothing to do with the fighting. The words had a different feel to them when a young American girl, the same age as Sarah, had copied them down so carefully in that battered, bloodstained notebook.

Sarah closed the book. Daisy, the American she never knew, had done so much more for Ireland, felt much more passionately about Ireland, than Sarah had ever done. Now she was dead. Hundreds of the rebels were dead, fighting for Irish freedom. She was angry at the way people had had to die just so that they could have their own government like England or America. She clutched the little book very tightly. She didn't want anyone to forget what Michael and Daisy had done. She didn't want their deaths to be in vain. She didn't want any of the deaths of that week and the weeks of executions that followed to be in vain.

She thought about her own part in the week of the rising. How she could have been killed, just walking past a window, how any one of them might have been killed, like the hundreds of innocent civilians who had been killed in the shooting, just crossing the road and going out trying to get hold of some food for their families. But she hadn't been killed. There must be a reason why she had survived when even this American girl, this girl she had never seen, had given her life for Ireland.

The final pages of the diary started with the day Daisy walked for hours through the streets of Dublin with the two women officers, trying to find food and finding only tragedy at every corner. They told of the fighting, the hope and good spirits inside the post office and the pride the rebels felt when they realized that such a small number of them had held out against the British army with all its heavy artillery for five days.

Sarah closed the black book with its red binding and the door opened.

'I've been looking all over the place for you and I can't stay.' Kitty moved to one side of the door. 'I know you're not meant to be on duty, but someone's come to say goodbye.'

Soldiers who were leaving the hospital at the castle were usually in full uniform. Often they were being sent straight back to join their regiments before going off to France again. But Diarmid was dressed in the civilian clothing his father had brought from the country. He still needed a stick to help him to walk.

'I am leaving to go back to the farm after lunch.' He looked taller now, in spite of the stick he needed to lean on. He stood just inside the door and said, 'You haven't been crying, have you, miss?'

Sarah shook her head. 'I've been reading the story of your brother's bravery. This is one of the things he had with him, a notebook from one of the other Volunteers, an American girl. Won't you sit down a minute?'

Diarmid sat down, hooking his stick over the back of one of the chairs round the table, and then held out his hand.

'Can I have the book?'

Sarah had only just read the last line: *I am handing this book and the revolver I've been given to Michael, a fellow Volunteer, for safe keeping. With God's help we will both come out of here alive.'*

She shook her head. 'I'll have to give the book to Daisy's mother.' She picked up the photo she had of Daisy and showed him and Diarmid frowned.

'That's something they shouldn't have done. They shouldn't have got women and girls involved in the fighting. War is no place for a girl.'

Sarah couldn't help smiling. 'This girl taught your brother how to shoot properly. Anyway, read the proclamation. It doesn't just talk of men. It calls to Irishmen and Irishwomen. All of us. And now we have to tell everyone about it, to keep their spirit alive.' And she showed him the page in the notebook where Daisy had copied down the proclamation.

'What will you do now? Will you go back to school?'

'I'm old enough to leave. Like Kitty.' Sarah was

159

annoyed at Diarmid for thinking she was still young. She stood up and started to sort out the cutlery they'd be needing for lunch, even though she wasn't on duty. 'But I shall go back to school. My father's coming to see me tomorrow. I'll tell him I need to stay on at school for some time, now. I've decided I want to be a doctor. Ireland needs doctors. He'll be surprised when I tell him I need to go back to school.' She had finished the cutlery and didn't know what to do next, so she wiped her hands on her apron and smiled. 'But I shan't go back to the school they sent me to in England.' She smiled again. 'I'm not English.'

She climbed on the chair again and got down the knapsack, with the first-aid tin and the metal bottle, putting them on the table beside Diarmid.

He picked up the knapsack.

'I gave him this to look after for me. It belonged to a German.' He opened up the tiny first-aid tin and closed it again and there was a long silence before he whispered, 'Was there a gun?'

He looked straight at Sarah. She couldn't lie to him.

'Is it here in the hospital?'

She shook her head. 'I took it so he wouldn't get into any more trouble. There was talk of them shooting all the rebels. That's why I said he was part of the British army. I didn't want them to shoot him.'

'Can you get the gun for me?'

Sarah shook her head. 'You don't need a gun any more. More guns means more killings. You've got to find a better way, a way to get freedom without guns.'

'Every free country in the world has an army. Every free country has the right to have an army to defend itself. And an army can't call itself an army if it has no guns. Freedom means an army and guns. I'll be needing my brother's gun.'

'But you're in the British army.'

Diarmid shook his head. 'They won't want me now, now I can't walk fast enough. And I won't be part of them any more. They shot my brother.'

His voice was getting louder and Sarah grabbed at his wrist to try and make him be quiet. 'You don't know who you can trust,' she said. 'They're still arresting people.' Then she smiled and whispered, 'How do you even know you can trust me?'

He spoke quietly.

'Because you told lies to try to save my brother. Because you hid his gun to try and save him. Because you didn't lie to me about it.' Then he whispered. 'There are plenty of people I can trust. There are more of us than you know. There are people joining up already, in this hospital. We'll go quietly now. We'll go quietly back to our farms and our jobs. And we'll get our strength back. But things have changed now. Things will never go back to the way they were before the rising.'

Diarmid opened and closed the first-aid tin, pressing hard on the centre of the lid with its red cross before he put it into the knapsack.

'They say in all the papers that they've crushed the rebels, but they know the struggle isn't over yet. What they don't know is how many people, twice as many as before, have joined up after what they did to Connolly and the others. Things have changed. We don't hate the British. All we want is our own country and our own government. All we want is for Ireland to be free.'

He picked up the knapsack and turned to go. 'You will get my brother's gun for me, won't you?'

Sarah shook her head. 'I can't,' she said, 'I'm truly sorry. I just can't. And even if I could . . . ' She saw that he was about to argue with her. 'You're angry with them because they killed your brother. Whose brother will you kill if I get you the gun? And what will happen after that? There's been enough killing.'

She opened the door. 'I want Ireland to be free. Just like you. But first we have to be free of all this fear and killing.' She handed Diarmid his stick. 'Now your mother and father will be waiting.'

Also by Elizabeth Lutzeier

The Coldest Winter

ISBN 0 19 275202 2

'For pity's sake!' shouted Eamonn's father. 'The man's got five children. Leave him a roof over his head.'

But the English soldiers either couldn't understand Irish, or else someone had put a spell on them, freezing their hearts so that they couldn't feel any pity for the children who were going to have to sleep out in the cold fields.

It is 1846 in Ireland and the potato harvest has failed. When Eamonn and his father had started digging, the potato plants were all green, and a soft gentle rain had cleared the air. But overnight the potato blight poisoned everything and their food for the whole year had rotted.

English soldiers turned families out of their homes, the roads were full of people with nowhere to go, and there was no work. Ireland was no place for the living—not unless you had a lot of money and a big warm house.

This is the story of how Eamonn and his family tried to stay alive in spite of the cold and famine, and how, with the help of a young girl, Kate Burke, they tried to survive through the coldest winter Ireland had ever known.

'superbly written'
    Children's Books in Ireland

'Beautifully executed historical novel'
    Glasgow Herald

'The story, written from the child's view, is heartbreakingly painful to read'
    Yorkshire Post

'A poignant and compelling story that makes you feel empathy with all its characters'
    Bournemouth Daily Echo

Bound for America

ISBN 0 19 275167 0

'We'll soon be in America, the whole ship. Every one of us. And then nothing bad can happen any more.'

As the great ship sailed further and further away, Ireland melted to a grey ghost on the horizon. And Kate, her stepmother, and her grandfather—all the people who had helped Eamonn through the great famine—disappeared like ghosts do when the sun comes up. Bound for America, Eamonn knew he would never see his country or his friends again. They were going to a place where land was plentiful, where there were jobs for anyone who wasn't afraid of hard work. But will the reality live up to Eamonn's dreams, or are there more hardships and heartbreaks in store for them . . . ?

'a heart-rending story which will give you some idea of what life was really like for Irish immigrants in America 150 years ago. I thought the book was superb'
East Anglian Daily Times

'This is a gripping and heartfelt novel for ten year olds and above.'
The Tablet

'some excellently realized dramatic encounters'
Books for Keeps

'Elizabeth Lutzeier is a natural storyteller, keeping the reader in suspense until the very end.'
Bournemouth Daily Echo